CAMP '67

Brendan Whitt Copyright © 2016 The OPAL Beatrice

Creative Company

Camp '67 ebook edition August 2016

Camp '67 paperback edition August 2016

ISBN: 0692745017

ISBN-13:978-0692745014

DEDICATION

I would like to dedicate this novella to Molly Connaughton. To you I am forever grateful. And as always thanks to my family...

CHILDREN HAVE NEVER BEEN VERY GOOD AT
LISTENING TO THEIR ELDERS, BUT THEY HAVE NEVER
FAILED TO IMITATE THEM - JAMES BALDWIN

Brendan Whitt - Camp '67

CONTENTS

"Just Make Friends"

As Mr. Amoretti navigated his long bodied Lincoln Continental through the mid-afternoon traffic his son Nicky sat quietly in the back seat with his arms folded. The warm air continued to blow obnoxiously into Nicky's face through his open window. Nicky was shorter than most of the boys and even some of the girls in his grade. He didn't care much about his appearance or his hygiene. Mr. Amoretti was a rather large man with a thick mustache and a head full of graying hair that he kept manicured. He owned two small car lots, a smoke shop, and was preparing to open up a bar. Sitting in the passenger seat was his wife and Nicky's mother, Mrs. Amoretti. She was a very stunning woman for her age with brunette hair and a keen eye for fashion. While her husband worked Mrs. Amoretti played homemaker happily raising their family in a sumptuous suburban lifestyle. She was constantly checking on Nicky, her youngest of three sons through the passenger side mirror. The tension between her husband and youngest son was beginning to pester her.

"Nicky, why don't you give it up already?" she said.

9

"Because he's still a baby!" Mr. Amoretti yelled. "All of this goddamn money I'm spendin' so he can have a summer of fun and 'hope' and he's upset!"

"He wanted to spend some more time with Mike." Mrs. Amoretti said.

Nicky's oldest brother Luca was 25 years old and lived out of town with his wife and newborn son. The Amoretti's middle child Mike was preparing for his freshman semester at an out of state college in the fall. Nicky was very close to Mike and imitated everything he did. He looked up to his big brother like most boys would. Nicky wore the same jersey number Mike wore during his first year as a member of the town's junior high football team. Nicky's resemblance to Mike caused many of his teachers to mistakenly address Nicky by his older brother's name.

"Mike is gonna be workin' all summer long Nick." Mr. Amoretti said. "Ya hav'ta learn how to be your own man one day."

Mrs. Amoretti turned around in her seat and looked at Nicky who was still staring out of the window with his arms folded. "You can play all of the sports you do at home with your new friends."

"I don't have any friends at that place." Nicky said.

"Then make some new ones!" Mr. Amoretti said.

Mrs. Amoretti turned around in her seat and gave her husband a mean-looking scowl. Feeling the pressure from his wife's permeating stare Mr. Amoretti dropped the conversation. Everyone in the car sat in silence as the shiny long bodied Lincoln Continental continued down the seemingly never ending road.

All campers were to be dropped off at a designated high school near the county border. As Mr. Amoretti pulled into the parking lot all Nicky could think of was the fact that the next ten weeks of his summer would be spent at Camp Hope N' Oak. Nicky and his father began to unload Nicky's bags from the trunk. "Hey look," Mr. Amoretti said, "they really do have colored kids at this camp. "There's the 'hope' right there." he said as he chuckled. Mrs. Amoretti shot her husband a look of non-amusement.

"I'll go check him in." she said.

Nicky and his dad stood next to each other without speaking for several minutes. Finally, Mr. Amoretti looked at his son and noticed that Nicky was still upset with him. He let out a sigh before dropping to a knee to talk to his youngest son. "Listen Nick, I know you wanna spend time with Mike this summa'. I looked up to your Uncle Joe the same way you look up to Mike. "Nicky

11

looked his dad in the eye as he fought back a few tears. "But there comes a time when you have to let go and grow up. Just make friends. That's all you gotta do."

On the other side of the lot was Milton Williams. He was sitting with his mother as the other campers got to know each other. He was still tired from the walk he and his mother had taken from the final stop on the bus line. Milton was a tough thirteen year old who wore his hair in a short black afro. He liked to hear about the Black Panthers and all of the good they did for Black people, especially the youth out in Oakland. Milton's burgeoning thoughts were inspired by the likes of Huey Newton and the late Malcolm X.

"I don't wanna go wit' all these white kids. They ain't gon like me anyway." he said.

"You hush!" Ms. Williams snapped. "I didn't work all of those extra hours just for you to complain." Milton sank into his seat. He lived with his mother in a two bedroom apartment where he and his older brother Travis shared a room. Travis joined the Navy as a way to help take care of Milton and his mother. Travis was set to return home after finishing up a tour in Vietnam but deferred to continue fighting so that he could continue making money to support his family.

Ms. Williams picked up an extra job so she could afford to send Milton to Camp Hope N' Oak during the summer. Without Travis around Ms. Williams was having trouble keeping Milton in line. Most adults who knew Milton referred to him as a troubled child. He hung around a tough crowd from the neighborhood and his grades had been on a steady decline. "Most of your friends' mothers wouldn't even do this for them." Ms. Williams said.

Milton and Travis' father disappeared not long after Milton was born leaving his then eight-year-old brother as his acting father figure. With Travis a half a world away Milton was angry and alone. "When they call you to get on that bus you better be the first one in line. And don't forget that you are in cabin No.20."

Back on the other side of the lot Mr. Amoretti stood in silence with his dejected son as they both waited for Mrs. Amoretti to return to the car. "I gave them all of the emergency contact information and Nicky is all checked in." Mrs. Amoretti said. She looked down at Nicky who had a smudge on his right cheek. She licked her thumb and wiped it clean. "My god," she said, "I'm dreading how you'll look in August. Don't forget you're in cabin No.20 ok?" Nicky unenthusiastically shook his head yes.

"Well Nick. We'll see you in six weeks." Mr. Amoretti said as he gave his son a stern pat on the back. He got into the car and turned the ignition. Mrs. Moriarty gave Nicky a tight bear hug which she accompanied with a wet motherly smooch on his cheek leaving behind a pink lipstick mark.

"Have fun sweetheart." Mrs. Amoretti said. She got into the car as Mr. Amoretti honked his horn before pulling out of the lot. Nicky stood in the middle of the black top parking lot emotionless as he watched his dad's black Lincoln Continental drive away. As the majority of the parents began to leave, the accompanying counselors started a head count as they instructed everyone to get onto the buses in an orderly fashion. Nicky and Milton respectively grabbed their bags and began to board their bus.

Welcome to Camp
Hope N' Oak

Dear Parent\Guardian,

We at Camp Hope N' Oak would like to invite your child to join us this summer for our youth camp. Our mission is to turn your child's boring old summer into one of fun and acceptance. The world is an ever-changing place. Our current state as a country could be scary to most children. We look to give them an escape from the daily depictions of hate and violence in our news media.

Camp Hope N' Oak replaces the old Barrington All Boys Camp which had a very strict enrollment policy. No Jews and, no Blacks, or colored children of any descent. Camp Hope N' Oak is proud to say that we accept ALL campers regardless of their race or creed.

Our camp's amenities includes a Cafeteria with a full staff and endless possibilities. Our sports and recreation area features a baseball diamond and football field. Our leisure hall features a library, game room and multipurpose room for all daily scheduled activities. We even have our own man made lake for the campers

15

to cool down in during those scorching summer days.

Camp begins July 7th and will run through August 18th. Registration should be completed no later than June 7th. We hope to see your little camper join us for our inaugural summer as we let the hope shine in!!!

Sincerely,

Cathy Wilkes, Camp Director of Camp Hope N' Oak

The eager and excited campers of Camp Hope N' Oak sang and talked amongst themselves as the convoy of yellow school buses made its way down an old dirt road surrounded by dense forestry. Each bus had one male and female counselor to supervise the campers and make sure that none of them got too rowdy on their way to camp.

Camp Hope N' Oak was the brain child of Cathy Wilkes. Ms. Cathy as she liked to be called, was the widow of a very successful investment banker and business man. When he died Mr. Wilkes left his trophy wife his entire estate along with a very generous trust fund for their son. Ms. Cathy was a former beauty pageant contestant who was moved by the civil rights movement her and the rest of the country were witnessing. Compelled by Dr. Martin Luther King's "I Have a Dream" speech, Cathy Wilkes began working on plans for a place that children of all races could enjoy together.

Milton Williams was on Bus No.2. He wasn't used to being around so many white kids. Where Milton was from the only white people in his neighborhood were racist cops or shady politicians lying about what they would do for his community.

Sitting on the other side of the aisle two rows behind Milton was Nicky Amoretti. As Milton surveyed the bus he looked behind him. When he made eye contact with Nicky, Milton tried to give him a generous head nod to which Nicky responded with a scowl.

Nicky's reaction put Milton on the defensive. "What the hell is wrong with this kid?" Milton thought.

How could he feel comfortable when he was subjected to watching and hearing about his people being sprayed down by fire hoses while being attacked by police dogs on a constant basis? Now this white kid, who he did not know was making him feel unwelcome. "This is going to be a long six weeks." he muttered under his breath.

The campground that Camp Hope N' Oak sat on used to serve as a summer getaway exclusively for white boys from rich and prestigious families. The old owner Roger Barrington shut down operations shortly before dying of natural causes. The campground sat dormant and uninhabited for several years until Ms. Cathy bought up the land and repurposed the entire campground.

When campers first entered Camp Hope N' Oak they were greeted by two wooden totem poles that held the camp's handcrafted sign. Further down the trail were the cabins and counselor dorms. There was a total of 30 cabins split between the boys and girls. To the left were the girls' cabins No.1 - 15 and on the right were the boys' cabins No.16-30. Each cabin housed four campers and had two bunk beds, two four-shelf dressers, and a small restroom with a sink and toilet. There was also a small window in the bathroom to help with ventilation.

Sitting cater-corner from the cabins was the largest building at camp, the mess hall or "the mess" for short. Mr. Tommy was an older black man and the chef at Camp Hope N' Oak. His assistant chef Carl was also black. Breakfast was served daily from 8 to 9 a.m., lunch ran from noon until 1 p.m. and dinner was served from 6 to 7:30 p.m. the mess had everything a kid wanted their parents to make for dinner every night, but didn't. Pizza, burgers, brownies, ice cream, donuts, the mess had everything. Every other Friday was Fiesta Fridays where the mess served Mexican themed food like tacos, taco salads, fajitas, and burritos. Towards the back of the mess were huge metal vats of home made lemonade and iced tea. Some days the mess would even serve malts and shakes.

To the left of the mess was Ms. Cathy's office and to the right were the showers. Further down the path towards the back of camp was the man made Boddle Lake. The lake was open to campers from 10 a.m. to 4 p.m. every Monday, Wednesday, Friday and Saturday. Tuesdays, Thursdays and Sundays were organized activity days. If the temperature reached over 90 degrees the lake would be open regardless of what day it was.

Sitting behind the boys' cabin block was the football field and baseball\softball diamond. Next to the showers was the Leisure Hall. The Leisure Hall was a bit smaller than the mess and housed the game room, mini library and the organized activities room. The game room had ping pong, pool, and foosball tables along with a cabinet full of board games. There were five guy counselors and

19

five girl counselors who lived in dorms behind their respective cabin blocks. All ten of them were college students who worked at the camp as a summer job.

The average day went as follows, after morning announcements at 7:50 a.m. the campers had one hour to get to the mess and eat breakfast. Just like all other meals the options seemed limitless; eggs or omelets made to order, pancakes, waffles, or French toast topped with blueberries, strawberries, apples, or chocolate chips. There was ham, bacon, sausage patties and links. You could eat oatmeal, grits, cream of wheat, or go to the cold cereal bar.

From 9 until noon campers could go back to their cabin or they could go to the Leisure Hall for an organized activity. After lunch it was a free for all, just as long as you stayed out of trouble. After dinner only the Leisure Hall was open where a camper could enjoy a night activity or go back to their cabin and wait for "lights out" which was at 10 p.m. sharp. No lights on and no one was allowed to leave their cabin unless it was an emergency. Camp Hope N' Oak is what one would call orchestrated chaos, as long as you didn't leave camp grounds you were ok.

As the convoy pulled up to the camp's large wooden totem pole styled gate, all of the campers got quiet. Everyone stood up to look out of their windows. Standing outside was the beautiful Ms. Cathy. She had blonde hair and was wearing blush with bright pink lipstick. Behind her was her son Brad. Brad had dirty blonde hair and a muscular physique. In the distance the mess donned a hand-painted sign that stretched from one end of the building to the other that read, "Welcome to Camp Hope N' Oak!" with the point at the bottom of the exclamation mark stylized as a peace sign.

Nice to Meet You Too...

When the buses came to a complete stop their doors opened up as the counselors led the campers into the entrance. Ms. Cathy was wearing one of the biggest and brightest smiles that anyone had ever seen. Once all of the campers were off of the buses, the counselors who rode with the campers joined Ms. Cathy and her son Brad who looked older than all of the other counselors.

When Milton stepped off of the bus he instantly noticed that all of the counselors were white. He remained on high alert as if he was waiting for a riot to happen at any moment. He had seen a few other black faces peppered throughout the crowd but it wasn't enough to make him happy. Ms. Cathy raised a bullhorn up to her mouth.

"Hello Campers," she shouted. Ms. Cathy spoke with a slight southern drawl and worded everything she said as if she was answering the judges during one of her old beauty pageants. "I am so excited to have you all here as me and my staff welcome you all to Camp Hope N' Oak! For the next six weeks I look forward to helping you all learn the necessary and basic skills of having fun and being friends in a world divided."

The campers all looked unmoved. Milton who was still upset

22

about Nicky mean mugging him on the bus was deciding which one of the other black kids he wanted to make friends with. After scouring the crowd he spotted another black boy standing alone. "Hey you," he whispered. The kid looked around before pointing to himself. Milton nodded his head and waved him over. The boy walked over to join Milton.

"What's your name?" Milton said.

"Ralph." the kid answered.

"You see that kid Ralph?" Milton said while pointing to Nicky. "If he look at me one more time he a racist."

"What makes you say that?" Ralph said.

"'Cause, he was starin' at me the whole ride."

"That doesn't make him a racist." Ralph said.

Milton turned his face up in disdain. "Nigga, don't you know what's goin' on? They don't want us here. White folks can't stand us."

"They all don't hate us." Ralph said. He left Milton and went back to the area he was standing in before. Milton turned his attention back to Ms. Cathy and her bullhorn.

"So I hope we all can enjoy ourselves and our time here and go back home with new experiences and fun stories." When Ms. Cathy finished her welcome speech she handed the bullhorn over to her son, and head counselor Brad.

"Alright," he said, "I want everyone to look at their welcome

23

letters and find your cabin number at the bottom. If you don't have your letter me and the other counselors will help you find your cabin. cabins No.1 through 15 are the girl's cabins and cabins No. 16 through 30 are the boy's cabins." Ralph pulled his letter out of his pocket. He unfolded it and saw that he was assigned to cabin No.20. Ralph picked up his bags and followed the crowd of kids to the cabins.

All of the buildings at camp were made from wooden logs. As Ralph continued to search for his cabin he could hear someone yell out to him. "Hey man!", the voice said. When Ralph turned around he saw a tall skinny white kid with bucked teeth, long brown hair, and sandals walking towards him. "What cabin are you looking for?" the boy asked.

"cabin No.20", Ralph replied.

"Looks like we're cabin mates." Johnny flashed Ralph his letter. Johnny was also assigned to cabin No. 20. I'm Johnny Stapleton by the way." he said.

"Ralph Dickerson. Nice to meet you."
Johnny shook Ralph's hand as the two of them looked for their cabin together.

"You excited for camp?" Johnny said.

"Yeah. What about you?"

"I'm pretty excited. Heard this place is the bee's knees." Johnny said. As Johnny and Ralph became acquainted with one

24

another they stumbled upon their cabin. "Well we're here. cabin No.20." Johnny opened the door as Ralph followed behind him. Each cabin was medium sized with two bunk beds, two dressers (each with four drawers apiece), a chest at the foot of each bed, a screened window facing the front of the cabin, and a ceiling fan.

In the back of the cabin was a small bathroom with a sink and toilet. The bathroom had a small window for ventilation. One of the top bunks already had luggage on it. "Guess somebody else got here first." Johnny said. As Johnny and Ralph got situated the door swung open. It was Milton.

"So we cabin mates huh? Cool brotha, cool."

"Hey, I'm Johnny." When Johnny went to shake Milton's hand, Milton looked at Johnny as if he was contagious with a deadly disease. Milton smacked Johnny five before hopping onto the bed that he claimed.

"Hey Johnny," Ralph said, "you want top bunk or bottom bunk?"

"I'll take the top bunk."

"Ok." Ralph said.

Milton leaned over towards Ralph and whispered, "Shoulda took the top."

"I don't think it matters." Ralph said.

As everyone finished getting situated the last cabin mate walked in, Nicky Amoretti. "Aw hell naw!" Milton shouted. "Two of ya'll?"

"Two what?" Nicky said.

"White boys." Everyone in the cabin went silent. Milton stood with his chest poked out to assert his dominance. Johnny looked at Ralph who looked at Milton who was staring Nicky down. Nicky dropped his bags and walked up to Milton.

"I could tell I didn't like you on the bus." Nicky said.

"Why, 'cause I'm black?"

"I could care less about that. It's 'cause you look like you want trouble. That's why."

"Man I'll kick yo little ass." Before the war of words turned physical Ralph and Johnny stepped in between the two cabin mates.

Ralph grabbed Milton, "Let's take a walk." Ralph said. Johnny and Nicky stayed behind as Ralph followed an irate Milton out of the cabin. Milton felt comfortable around Ralph. He was calm, collected, and most importantly Black.

It was hard for Milton to accept the world around him. All he saw was a bunch of people who looked like Johnny and Nicky that hated people who looked like him and Ralph.

Back in the cabin Nicky was fuming with anger. Johnny who was also upset managed to keep his cool. Johnny was raised in a very liberal household. His father was a pro-Civil Rights lawyer and anti-war proponent. Johnny's mother was a pediatrician who ran a non-profit hospital that catered to destitute inner city residents. Johnny was raised to be accepting of all people. Johnny was better suited to understand Milton's anger than Nicky was. "You alright?," Johnny said.

"What's that kid's problem anyway. I ain't done nothin' to him."

"He's probably just upset about the stuff he sees on the news. It isn't his fault." Johnny said.

"Whatever. He comes at me like that again I'm gonna kick his ass!"

"And what will that solve?" Johnny said.

"His attitude problem." Johnny saw there was no reasoning with Nicky.

Ralph continued to try calming Milton down. Ralph was a very astute kid. He had two working class parents and a three-year-old sister. He wasn't oblivious to what was going on in the world around him. With both of his parents being college educated they taught and reminded Ralph about his history constantly.

The neighborhood he and his family lived in had a handful of white families. Ralph knew all whites weren't like the images on the news and in the paper. He wanted Milton to calm down not only because it was the right thing to do, but because it was going to keep peace in the cabin during the summer. "Why are you so angry?" Ralph said.

"My brother told me we ain't even supposed to be here. They brought us over here just to treat us like shit. They think we all the same so Ima treat them like they all the same."

"But they aren't." Ralph said.

"Nigga they got you brainwashed. You even sound like them." Milton pushed his way past Ralph. He watched Milton storm off into a sea of campers. Ralph turned around and headed back to the cabin to check on Johnny's progress with Nicky. When he got back Nicky was laying down on the bunk Milton claimed while Milton's bags sat on the floor. Nicky was reading a comic book while Johnny sat on his bunk writing in a notebook. Ralph walked to his bunk and laid down. A minute later Johnny hung his head over the edge of his bunk as his hair dangled. "Did you get him to calm down?" he said. Ralph shook his head no. "We can try again later. Let's head to the mess. Dinner should be ready in another half hour or so." Johnny looked over at Nicky. "You wanna join us?," he said.

"No," Nicky mumbled.

Ralph and Johnny headed to the mess leaving Nicky to decompress on his own. The boys hadn't even been at camp for a full hour and there had already been a conflict within the cabin. If they couldn't solve their differences between themselves, cabin No.20 was in for a long and agonizing six weeks together.

Suddenly Johnny thought of a solution. "Maybe we should

bring them together." he said. "I mean, think about it. We get along and they don't. Let's play peacekeeper man." Ralph didn't like conflict but he didn't like playing mediator either. His father's philosophy was, "If it ain't your problem, don't try and fix it." He most often heard his father mutter that line whenever he watched Walter Cronkite report on America's involvement in Vietnam. The twelve-year-old wanted to apply that same logic to his current situation.

"I say we let them solve it themselves," Ralph said.

"C'mon man don't feed me that. You mediated when you took Milton for a walk." Johnny said.

"That was different. They were ready to swing on each other."

"And who says it won't happen again?"

Ralph knew Johnny was right. Maybe it was he and Johnny's job to make peace in the cabin. If they didn't then another altercation was imminent. Ralph considered Johnny his friend after only a couple of hours together. He was a cool and easygoing kid much like Ralph. If anyone could calm Milton down it was Johnny even if he was white.

"So after dinner we'll sit them down and pow-wow." Johnny said. "Until then let's venture around the camp." Johnny gave Ralph a pat on the back which in turn gave Ralph a feeling of reassurance.

While he and Johnny continued to tour around the camp Ralph

was amazed at its size. His parents told him it that the camp was big but he didn't know it would be this big. Johnny and Ralph's tour of the camp took Ralph's mind off of what transpired in the cabin earlier.

"So now what?" Ralph said.

"We can go back to the cabin and read comics or we can hang out here." Johnny said.

"Let's just chill out here." Ralph didn't really want to go back to the cabin. Not because of the tension. That was far from his mind. Ralph was enjoying the scenery around camp. Everywhere he looked he saw green. Ralph hadn't seen this much forestry since he and his parents went to a family reunion in Georgia before his sister was born. There was nothing but trees for as far as he could see and the air smelled fresh and clean. Ralph and Johnny sat quietly in a patch of grass as they soaked in the beautiful scenery.

A few moments later Milton saw Johnny and Ralph sitting in the grass as the two of them laughed and joked together. Something inside of Milton made him feel guilty about the way he lashed out at Johnny. He knew the best thing for him to do was to apologize for the way he acted. Milton walked over to Ralph and Johnny and sat down with them.

"Hey man, you cool now?" Johnny said.

"Yeah I'm cool." Milton said as he gave Johnny a fist bump.

"Can you and Nicky be cool?"

"I can try." Milton said.

Johnny was elated "Awesome!" he said with a huge smile. "Let's go grab some grub. I'm starving." The three of them got up and walked to the mess. Camp Hope N' Oak was progressive in the way they operated. After every meal the campers were told to dump their unfinished food and scraps into buckets. When it was almost time to leave, the counselors weighed up the total waste from all of the campers. Ms. Cathy used the "waste buckets" as a way to help teach the campers how to not be wasteful of food. Of course when given the options of their favorite foods the majority of the campers' eyes were a bit bigger than their stomachs.

After Ms. Cathy finished her spiel about not wasting food, Brad and the counselors all marched around the mess as they sang the camp's welcome song. When they were all finished it was time to eat. It wasn't until they were almost done eating that Ralph, Johnny, and Milton realized that Nicky never showed up for dinner. When everyone was finished Ms Cathy made another announcement.

She grabbed her bullhorn and turned it on as the feedback garnered everyone's attention. "Tonight before we all go to bed there will be an ice social in the Leisure Hall where we will be serving root beer floats. See you all tonight!" After Ms. Cathy's announcement the campers were dismissed back to their cabins. When the boys got back to their cabin Nicky was still laying down on the top bunk that Milton had claimed for himself. He continued to read his comics as if no one had walked through the door. It didn't take long for Milton to notice that his luggage was sitting on the ground.

"Hey man what you doin' on the top bunk?" Milton said. Nicky didn't bat a lash. Johnny and Ralph stood by hoping the exchange wouldn't escalate past words. "Nicky, why are you on my bunk?"

Nicky looked at Milton, "What does it look like kid, I'm readin'."

Milton's head jerked backed as he scrunched his face up. The moment of tension was the equivalent of watching Mt. Vesuvius prepare to erupt. Milton walked over to the bed as Johnny followed closely behind him.

"Let's keep this peaceful guys," Johnny said.

"Kid?" Milton said. "Nigga I got a name, and it's Milton." When he got to the bed, Milton grabbed Nicky's left leg and yanked him down from the top bunk. The comic book that Nicky was reading flew up into the air as his body went crashing onto the floor. Milton mounted him and began a ground and pound attack. All Nicky could do was guard his face. The situation had escalated so quickly that Ralph and Johnny had no time to react. Johnny went to break up the quarrel before Ralph grabbed him.

"Let them fight." Ralph said.

Milton continued to wail on Nicky who finally found an opportunity to throw a punch at Milton. Nicky may have been short but he was tough. Having two older brothers aged eighteen and twenty-five gave Nicky more than his fair share of wrestling matches. As a successful business owner Mr. Amoretti constantly preached, "Don't take shit from nobody. Amorettis don't do that." Had Johnny broken up the fight he was liable to catch a few punches from Nicky himself.

Nicky and Milton continued to tussle between the beds as they landed punches to each other's bodies and faces. The exchange was nothing short of a miniature Greco-Roman gladiator duel. Johnny, unable to take anymore of it grabbed Milton assuming he was more likely to throw a cheap shot had he grabbed Nicky.

"Alright guys enough!" Johnny said angrily. Both boys had blood on their faces which had gotten onto each others shirts. "You guys got it all out now?" Johnny said as he continued to restrain Milton.

Nicky wiped the blood from his lower lip. "Yeah I'm good," he said.

Johnny released Milton. "You good?" he said. Milton agreed with a head nod. "Good, I hope this fight got everything out of you two. We have to live here together for six weeks. Nicky, you can have my bunk."

Nicky calmly walked over and grabbed his bags. He turned to

Milton and put his hand out for a handshake. "Anybody who can sock me like that is alright." Milton shook Nicky's hand before picking up the comic he was reading and handing it to him. Ralph and Johnny went to their bunks to lay down. Johnny looked at Ralph. "Now we can just get along." he said.

"I hope so." Ralph replied.

As the sun continued to set behind the trees so did the tension in the cabin. After a tumultuous first day the cabin mates could finally enjoy their summer at Camp Hope N' Oak.

We All Ain' t the Same

A calm morning breeze swept its way through camp. The sun settled nicely behind the surrounding trees creating a picturesque morning. The smell of fresh air comforted each waking camper as a bugle horn played over the camp's speaker system. Ms. Cathy began to read that morning's announcements.

"Good morning campers!" Ms. Cathy shouted. "Today will be our first full day of camp. I hope you all continue to get to know each other as the week progresses and you begin to forge new friendships." It was hard to sleep through Ms. Cathy's chipper but imprudent wake up call. Ralph, who was the early bird of cabin No.20 was already awake and getting dressed. Johnny slowly got himself out of bed as Milton and Nicky continued to sleep. After Ralph got dressed he and Johnny headed to the mess for breakfast.

A short while later Nicky woke up as he rubbed the sleep from his eyes. "Where is everybody?" he said.

Milton didn't move a muscle. Nicky walked over to the window and saw campers were still pouring into the mess. Nicky decided to let Milton sleep as he got dressed to go eat breakfast. Halfway out of the door Nicky had a change of heart and turned around to wake Milton up. "Hey Milton," he said, "it's 8:30. You

35

don't wanna miss breakfast do you?." Milton opened his eyes and saw Nicky standing over him. When Milton turned over Nicky left him be.

After Nicky got his food he looked around the mess to see if he could spot Johnny or Ralph. When he couldn't find them Nicky took a seat at an empty table. "Mind if we site here?" someone said. Nicky turned around and saw boy identical twins standing behind him.

"Sure," Nicky said. The twins sat down with their food and began eating with Nicky.

Breakfast was almost over by the time Milton made his way to the mess. He grabbed a bowl of cereal and made his way to a table in the back. Before he could sit down Milton was spotted by Ralph and Johnny who waived him over to their table. They were sitting with another black kid.

"You actually made it." Ralph said. "Did you see Nicky around?."

"Not since he tried wakin' me up?" Milton said. "Who this?"

"Hello, I'm Dennis." the other kid said. Dennis wore a low haircut, was over dressed for summer camp, well groomed, and spoke proper English. He reminded Milton of Ralph but more refined.

Dennis stretched his hand out to Milton for a handshake. Milton took a moment to size Dennis up. He couldn't place his finger on it but Milton knew he didn't like Dennis. He hesitantly shook Dennis' hand before starting on his bowl of cereal.

"Well me and Dennis are headed to the leisure Hall." Ralph said. "Feel free to join us later."

Johnny gave Ralph a smile and a head nod. "Sure thing man." he said. As Ralph and Dennis left the mess, Milton followed Dennis out of the door with his eyes.

"I don't like him." Milton said.

"Just like you didn't like Nicky?" Johnny said.

"Nicky caught me in a bad mood. This kid just don't seem right."

Across camp Ralph and Dennis made their way over to the Leisure Hall. Ralph couldn't help but notice all Dennis did was talk about himself the entire walk. Dennis barely let Ralph get a single word in. He bragged about how good his grades were and how prestigious his school was. He bragged about his father's chain of grocery stores and all of the things his mother bought him. In the short hour Ralph had spent with Dennis, he knew about as much about Dennis as he did his own cabin mates.

"So what game do you want to play first?" Dennis said.

"I like foosball." Ralph answered.

"How about monopoly?"

"That game takes a little too long to play." Ralph said. "Besides it's only fun when you have more people."

While Ralph and Dennis tried to compromise on a game to play Nicky walked through the door. He was wearing a pair of ratty jeans and Mike's old junior high football jersey. He made his way over to where Ralph and Dennis were sitting to join them.

"Hey Dickerson what's up?" Nicky said.

"Nothing much." Ralph turned to Dennis, "This is one of my cabin mates Nicky."

Dennis sized up Nicky. "Nice to meet you. I'm Dennis."

"Guess I'll hang out here with you guys." Dennis who was used to being prim and proper took a look at Nicky's clothes. It didn't help that Nicky had worked up a sweat playing a quick game of football. The longer Dennis sat next to Nicky the more uncomfortable he became. He tried turning his head, holding his breath, and even hiding his nose inside of shirt. Dennis decided he had enough of Nicky's pungent body odor. He took it upon himself to inform Nicky about his stench.

"Do you shower often?" Dennis said.

"Ususally when my ma says. Why?"

"I think you need one." Dennis said.

Nicky instantly took offense to Dennis' suggestion. "Last time I checked, you ain't my ma." Nicky said. "What kind of pansies you hang around Dickerson?"

"I didn't know practicing good hygiene was a part of being a pansy." Dennis said in a snarky tone. "The showers are next door by the way."

Nicky stood up and began to yell at Dennis. "The only person who tells me I stink is my ma!" he said. "I don't see her here so who gives a shit about what you think?" The room went silent as everyone's focus shifted towards the area where Nicky, Ralph, and Dennis were sitting. When Nicky looked up he realized everyone in the room was looking at him. "Fuck this, I'm outta here." Nicky stormed out of the room as the other campers went back to what they were previously doing. Ralph was beginning to rethink his burgeoning friendship with Dennis. Dennis was pompous and rude. Ralph bit his tongue and kept his feelings to himself seeing as how he wasn't the type to badmouth a person.

Later that night after lights out Milton and Nicky were still up talking. Unbeknownst to them Ralph was still awake. He was having a hard time going to sleep. He had eaten too many brownies at dinner and was combating a bothersome stomach ache. Ralph chimed in on Nicky and Milton's conversation when he heard his name come up.

"Did you meet that kid Dickerson hangs out with?" Nicky said.

"I don't like him." Milton said.

"He told me I should take a shower? Who says that to somebody they just met?"

"If Dennis say somethin' to me crazy I'm beatin' his ass. No

39

questions asked."

"I might even help." Nicky said.

As the first week drew to a close everyone and everything at camp began to settle in. Campers from other cabins began to mingle with each other as they all began to catch the swing of things and how Hope N' Oak operated. One morning after breakfast Ralph and Johnny went to get changed into their swim trunks for a dip in the lake.

As they finished getting ready there was a knock at the door. It was Dennis. "Where you guys headed?" he said.

"We're headed to the lake for a swim." Ralph said. He was thinking of a way to get Dennis to take the hint that he didn't want to hang out with him anymore.

"Mind if I tag along?" Dennis said.

Ralph looked back to Johnny who simply shrugged his shoulders. The difference between Ralph and Milton was that Milton had no problem telling you he didn't like you. That way he could go on with his day and so could you. Ralph was a lot more passive in his approach. "Sure, I don't mind." Ralph said. He had faltered. Ralph turned back to Johnny, "That cool with you?" he asked.

"It's fine with me." Johnny said. Johnny was unaware of Dennis' encounter with Nicky. Even if he knew, Johnny was a peaceful soul. Johnny would have tried to mediate the exchange.

Accompanied by Dennis, Johnny and Ralph grabbed their things and went to the lake.

Milton on the other hand was becoming bored with camp. It wasn't fun to him. He was constantly trying to find something to get into. In his mind he could have stayed home and played football everyday. Milton found a large tree and took a seat as he leaned his back against it's thick trunk. On the other side of the tree two female counselors were talking. Milton chimed in on their conversation. As the two counselors talked about their plans for the night Milton's ears perked up.

"So is anyone going out to the woods tonight?" one of them asked.

"I think I heard one of the guys mention it but I'm not for sure." the other counselor said.

"Well even if we are going we'd have to wait for these little brats to go to sleep."

Milton waited until both of the counselors left before emerging from behind the tree. His summer was beginning to turn into the type of summer he was hoping for.

Over at the lake Ralph and Johnny were still enjoying the water. Dennis who voluntarily followed them to the lake hadn't touched the water once. Ralph noticed it but decided not to say anything. While Ralph struggled to figure out why Dennis followed him to the lake, Johnny had been constantly making eye contact with a girl. She was very pretty but he couldn't gather up enough courage to talk to her. Johnny waived to her prompting the brunette girl to wave back. Oblivious to Johnny becoming smitten with his new crush Ralph asked Johnny what he thought about Dennis.

"He's been in that same spot all day." Ralph said. "He hasn't even talked to anybody else."

"Maybe he's waiting on us to leave." Johnny said.

"It's weird. Why follow someone to the lake and not get in the water?"

"Good point." Johnny said

Ralph and Johnny got out of the lake and grabbed their things before heading back to the cabin. "Hey Dennis" Ralph said, "me and Johnny are headed back to our cabin. We'll catch up with you later."

"Then I'll see you at lunch." Dennis said. Ralph had hoped Dennis would get the message that he didn't want to hang out with him anymore that day. When Ralph and Johnny got back to the cabin Milton and Nicky were already there.

"Where's your boyfriend?" Milton said jokingly.

"I gotta find a way to get that kid to leave me alone." Ralph said.

"So that prissy ass nigga finally gettin' to you?"

"Well it's official" Nicky said, "we all hate him."

42

Johnny stood up and took the floor, "Hold on guys. We can't just hate a person because of who he is."

"Shit, why not?" Milton said.

"Because it's wrong." Johnny protested.

Milton walked over to Johnny and placed his arm around him. "Johnny listen, all niggas ain't the same."

"Because of how he talks and dresses?" Johnny said.

"Look, you don't get it and I'm hungry. I'm goin' to the mess."

When cabin No.20 got to the mess they all followed Nicky to a table where his two newest friends, the Ricketts twins were sitting. Nicky liked Dylan and David. Although Dylan was the better athlete both twins loved football just as much as Nicky did. If Nicky wasn't with his cabin mates then he was sure to be around one of the twins if not both.

After lunch everyone dispersed and went in search of something to do to occupy their time. Milton noticed Dennis from across the mess. He gave Ralph a nudge on the shoulder and pointed to Dennis with his head. Ralph paid Dennis no mind.

When cabin No.20 and the Ricketts twins got outside everyone went their separate ways. David and Dylan followed Nicky back to the field while Johnny went off on his own. Milton and Ralph walked around for a bit. After a while Milton noticed Dennis had been following him and Ralph since they left the mess. He turned around to confront Dennis. "Damn nigga, what you followin' us for?"

"I can walk wherever I want." Dennis said.

Milton stepped to the side. "Then walk past us." he said.

"I go when I want to go." Milton stood his ground as did Dennis. There weren't enough campers around to cause a big scene.

"Why you wanna be around so bad. Ralph don't even like you. Nicky don't like you and I hate you."

"I'm not very fond of ghetto niggers like you." Dennis said.

Ralph's eyes grew big. He remembered the first day of camp when Nicky and Milton came to bloody blows in the middle of their cabin floor just because Nicky referred to Milton as "kid". Milton took one step before leaning in with a strong right hook. Dennis hit the ground almost immediately.

Unknown to Milton, Ralph, Dennis, and the four or five spectating campers Brad watched the entire exchange. Just as Milton began to mount Dennis to unleash a flurry of blows Brad grabbed Milton and pulled him up off of Dennis. Ralph helped Dennis up who snatched away. "Alright. That's enough." Brad said. "You two come with me. Everybody else get out of here."

Brad led Milton and Dennis away. "What are you names?" he said.

"Milton."

"Milton what?"

"Milton Williams"

Brad turned his attention to Dennis. "And yours?"

"Dennis Worthy."

"Alright Milton and Dennis, I'm not going tell Ms. Cathy because she's had to enough deal with this week. So Milton I want you to go to your cabin and chill out. I'll come get you when I think you're ready. Dennis, I'm going take you to get an ice pack and then you're going do the same. Got it?" Both boys nodded in agreeance. "Now shake and make up." Dennis reached his hand out as Milton reluctantly did the same.

St. Agatha's

Milton could consider himself lucky. His fight with Nicky had been kept a secret between only him and his cabin mates which in turn brought everyone in the cabin closer together. His fight with Dennis had also been kept a secret after Brad decided to handle the matter himself. Ms. Cathy had enough to deal with after the first week of camp. There was a fight in one of the girls' cabins, a bully whose cabin mates exacted revenge in the form of water boarding, and one camper was bullied about his body odor to the extent that his parents had to pick him from camp.

Dennis had become an afterthought to Milton once he and Nicky finally had the chance to talk about the "Counselor's Hangout". Like Milton, Nicky was also becoming bored with Camp Hope N' Oak's mundane daily schedule. The idea of going on an adventure at night was more than enough to convince Nicky to tag along. Their biggest hurdle would be learning the surrounding area. Neither of them had any navigation skills or knew much about the wilderness.

One afternoon as the mess cleared out after lunch Nicky and Milton went back to the cabin. Nicky pulled out a piece of paper and laid it out on his bed. It was a hand drawn map of the entire camp. Nicky included the entrance, counselor's quarters, and the cabins. the mess was right where it should be along with the lake and field. There were red and black X's marked at various locations around camp.

"Remember when you told me about the place counselors go when everyone goes to sleep?" Nicky said. "This is the map that's gonna get us there."

"How?" Milton asked.

"Once we understand how to get out of the camp finding out where the counselors go is the next step."

Milton took a moment to process what Nicky was saying. "So what do the red and black X's mean?"

"Red means danger zones and black means blind spots."

Milton was confused. "Blind spots for what?"

"One night I stayed up to see what goes on when everybody's sleepin'. Two counselors patrol the cabins before switchin' off. The blind spots are where they don't patrol."

The danger zones were mostly the cabins and the mess while the blind spots were everything beyond those points. Milton liked where Nicky was going with his plan. He decided that he and Nicky should prepare for their "mission" as soon as possible.

One afternoon while Ms. Cathy was out of her office, Nicky snuck in and took a flashlight. The two boys figured Ms. Cathy would never grow suspicious of the missing flashlight since the counselors were constantly in and out of her office throughout the day. Milton and Nicky alternated between who stayed up and watched the counselors. They logged shift changes down on paper using Ralph's watch as he slept.

After a few nights of watching and logging, Nicky and Milton had detailed records of the counselors' patrols along with Nicky's hand drawn map of the camp. With everyone adjusted to the flow of camp it was easy for a camper to go off and do his or her own thing. Nicky and Milton had to keep their mission a secret between only the two of them. The slightest leak would compromise the entire operation. The only decision left to be made was whether or not they were going to tell Ralph and Johnny about their mission.

"Should we tell them?" Nicky said.

Milton thought long and hard about it before answering. "I don't know." he said.

"Let's tell them later on today and see what they say." Nicky suggested.

Milton didn't really want to tell anyone else about the plan. He figured that was the easiest way to have a leak. On the other hand having two more people help out would make finding the counselor's hangout a lot easier. He figured Johnny wouldn't mind joining him and Nicky for the mission. Milton had his doubts about Ralph on the other hand. He was passive and a bit of a goody two shoes in Milton's opinion. "I don't know about Ralph," he suggested.

"What do you mean?" Nicky said.

"He might be too scared to go along."

"Then we'll leave him behind if we have to. I know he won't snitch." Nicky said. Milton was beginning to wonder if telling Nicky about the hangout was a good idea.

That evening before dinner Nicky and Milton were still contemplating on whether or not to include Johnny and Ralph into their plan. Nicky who was growing more and more anxious by the second looked over at Milton. "Hey Milton," he said in a failed whisper, "should we tell 'em?"

Johnny who overheard Nicky's loud whispering looked up. "Tell us what," he said.

Milton let out a groan, "Now we gotta tell 'em."

Milton reluctantly got up and stood by the door to keep watch for anyone who got close enough to overhear their conversation. Johnny and Ralph sat on Johnny's bunk as Nicky pulled his hand drawn map from under his pillow. Ralph and Johnny confusingly looked at each other. "Milton heard a few counselors talk about this place they go after lights out a few days ago."

"What is it?" Johnny said.

"Some place in the woods." Milton answered.

"And me and Milton came up with a plan." Nicky unfolded his map spreading it out between Johnny and Ralph. "This is us," he said pointing to their cabin. "These are the places the counselors patrol at night, and these are the blind spots."

"Tonight we goin' on a mission to scope out the surroundin' area," Milton said.

Ralph stood up, "I like to have as much fun as the next kid but sneaking out, getting caught, and possibly kicked out isn't worth it."

"Let's think on it." Johnny said. "I mean they do have a plan. Now they have two more heads to help carry it out." Johnny wanted everyone to go on the mission. In his mind it was another way to keep everyone in the cabin together.

"I'm not doing it." Ralph said.

Milton looked over at Nicky, "I told you he was gon be scared. Shoulda' just kept yo mouth shut." Milton stormed out of the cabin slamming the cabin's thin screen door behind him. Nicky folded up the map and stuffed it back under his pillow.

"Look if you don't go I'll stay with you, but for now let's just go get some food," Johnny said. Ralph didn't have much of an appetite anymore. If he said no then Milton and Nicky would probably look at him differently. If he said yes then he ran the risk of getting caught and sent home. The pressures of making and keeping new friends at camp was beginning to get to Ralph.

During dinner Milton sat and ate with his friend Lawrence who one of the other dozen or so black campers. Ralph sat in silence and ate a light dinner while he rethought his decision. Sure the mission was risky, but at least he would have his friends with him. When the boys got back to the cabin they knew they only had a matter of hours until lights out. Ralph continued to go back and forth with himself on whether to join the mission or not. While on their way back from that night's activity at the Leisure Hall Johnny made one more attempt to convince Ralph to join the mission.

"C'mon Ralph, why not?" Johnny said.

"My dad paid a lot of money for me to be here. What if we get caught?"

"We get in trouble, go home, and tell our friends how far out it was."

Johnny made the offer sound so tempting. Maybe it was Ralph's subconscious or maybe it was Johnny's care free attitude. Ralph took a moment to think about it. "Alright, I'll go" he said, "but only because I don't want to be bored all night knowing you guys are out there."

"Awesome. So glad you're coming with us." Johnny said as he threw his arm around Ralph's shoulder.

After lights out the boys all hopped into their beds as if they were going to sleep. One by one as they did every night, the on shift counselors checked all of the cabins. When the counselor made his way to cabin No.20 everyone remained still and silent. The counselor took a peek inside with his flashlight before moving

51

on to the next cabin. After a couple of minutes Nicky and Milton jumped down from their bunks. Johnny swung his bed sheet back before going to cover the door. "He's almost gone," he whispered. Ralph sat on the edge of his bed as he tried to collect himself and calm his nerves.

Milton grabbed Ralph's backpack that he and Nicky had prepared for the mission. Everyone grabbed whatever they could find to stuff under their sheets so that when the counselor made his way back around it would appear that the boys were still in bed sleeping. When the counselor was out of sight Johnny and Milton snuck out of the front door of the cabin. Ralph took a moment to gather himself before following behind them. Seeing as how he was the only one small enough to climb out of the back window Nicky stayed inside and locked the door behind everyone else.

When Nicky finally squeezed his way through the bathroom window the boys looked around to make sure the coast was clear. Using the shadows cast by the camp's floodlights, cabin No.20 stealthily made their way over to the Leisure Hall. They waited for a moment before taking off into the woods.

Everyone kept running until the lights from camp were no longer visible. The boys stopped for a breather. The trees that surrounded them reached far into the sky. The leaves were thick and plentiful enough that they nearly blocked all of the moon's light. Milton went into the backpack and pulled out a flashlight he had stolen from Ms. Cathy's office.

"So where do we go next?" Milton said.

"I don't know," Nicky responded. "Let's just walk around until we find something."

Ralph who was against going on the mission in the first place was beginning to grow concerned. He followed his cabin mates out into the middle of the woods and none of them had any clue of where they were going.

"Let's just head back to camp and try this some other day," Ralph said.

"You can turn around and go back, I'm keepin' on," Milton said.

"Me too." Nicky added.

As Milton and Nicky continued forward Ralph looked to Johnny hoping he would side with him. Johnny simply shrugged his shoulders before proceeding to follow behind Milton and Nicky. With no flashlight or much of a choice, Ralph followed behind Johnny. There was an overcast that had begun to move in a little after dinner. Heavily dependent on the flashlight Milton continued to lead the way.

"Hey Nicky," Milton said, "this whak ass map ain't helpin'."

"My map was only supposed to get us to the woods, not lead us through." Nicky said.

"That's why Harriet Tubman ran the underground railroad.

White people never know where they goin."

"You do know Harriet Tubman didn't do it all by herself right?" Ralph said.

"Man whatever. Point is we lost 'cause of Nicky."

"Don't blame this on me" Nicky said. The boys were clearly lost.

In the midst of their bickering Johnny shushed Nicky and Milton. "You see what I see" he said. In the distance past the trees the boys could see what looked like lights up ahead.

"Look like it's a town or somethin' past the trees." Nicky said.

The boys continued to push forward towards the unknown source of light. When they reached the tree line the boys could see a church sitting in the middle of what looked liked a another camp. There was a building that looked liked the Leisure Hall back at camp and what looked like two large multi-roomed houses that sat across from each other. As the boys slowly emerged from the tree line they looked around for a sign or something that could tell them where they were. The sign in front of the church read "St. Agatha's Summer Christian Camp".

"My grandma lives close to a school by that name" Johnny said. "I'm pretty sure this is the same one. It's an all girls Catholic school."

Milton turned his attention to Johnny. "So you tellin' me we just found a camp full of girls?"

"If it's the St. Agatha's I know then yeah." Johnny said.

"Then let's keep on." Milton said ecstatically.

As the boys made their way through the calm and quiet campus, Ralph was becoming increasingly unnerved. He checked his watch and saw that it was now past midnight. After finding out the map was pretty much useless Ralph wasn't sure if Nicky and Milton had clocked the counselors patrol schedules accurately.

He didn't want to be unlucky enough to be sneaking back into camp at the same time the counselors were doing another walkthrough. Suddenly there was a tap on the window of the house on the left. The tap startled the boys causing them all to jump. There was a girl with long red hair wearing an all white night gown. She was directing the boys to walk to the back of the house.

"Should we trust her?" Nicky said.

"We don't really have a choice at this point." Johnny said.

Nicky and Ralph hid on the side of the house as Johnny and Milton walked to the back. When Milton and Johnny made their way to the back of the house they waited for the girl to let them in. She opened the door and poked her head through.

"What the hell are you doing here?" she asked.

"I'm Johnny and this is Milton."

"Where are the other two?" the girl said.

"They're on the side of the house. We got lost in the woods and were hoping-."

"Shut up and get in here before you get caught. If Sister Mary sees you we're all in trouble."

Johnny poked his head around the corner signaling Ralph and Nicky to come around back. Once inside, the girl led the boys into the dining room. There was a long oak table with ten chairs to each side. "Stay here," she said. They all took a seat as the girl went into another room.

"This a big ass house," Milton said.

"We gotta get going," Ralph interjected, "It's after midnight."

"We gotta figure out how to get back first." Milton said. "Did you see her nipples through that gown though?

"I did." Johnny said. "Nice and perky."

When the girl came back into the room everyone went quiet. "First off where did you come from?" she said.

Ralph looked at Milton who looked at Nicky. Nicky looked at Johnny hoping he could give the girl an answer. "We were sneaking around the woods and got lost." Johnny said.

The redhead was suspicious. She took a seat at the head of the table. "Why'd you come here?" she said.

Everyone continued to sit in silence in hopes that Johnny would continue answering questions as the group's representative. "We saw lights and went towards them I guess."

"You guys are idiots. If Beth caught you guys she would've told." the girl said.

"Numb nuts over here got us lost." Milton said

Nicky snapped back. "You're the one who came up with this half assed plan." he said in a loud tone.

"Can you guys keep quiet," the girl whispered. "You're going to get me and yourselves into a lot of trouble. Now where did you guys come from?

"Camp Hope N' Oak," Johnny said.

The girl let out a sigh, "Your camp isn't that far." she said. "You've probably been going around in a circle. Just go straight through the woods. If you don't get turned around you should be back in no time."

"Thanks," Johnny said . "What's your name by the way?"

"Just get the hell out of here before I get in trouble. This is a Catholic all girls camp you know."

"Well, guys let's get going, and thanks again." Jess rolled her eyes as the boys went out through the back door. When they got to the tree line a flashlight shined in their direction as an older woman shouted. "Who are you? You better get out of here!" The boys all took off running into the woods.

Everyone's heart was racing as they continued to run deeper and deeper into the thick forest. When the boys knew they were far enough from St. Agatha's everyone stopped to catch their breaths. Milton handed the flashlight over to Johnny who led the group back to camp.

Comrades

One morning as the campers continued to sleep Ms. Cathy gathered all of the boys counselors into her office. A short while later she made an announcement over the camp's speaker system. "Attention All Campers." she said. She didn't sound like her usual warm and bubbly self. "This announcement is only for cabins No.16 through 30. Please report to the field immediately. I repeat, please report to the field immediately."

Not long after Ms. Cathy made her announcement all of the male counselors began going door to door to wake up any of the boys who were still asleep. Having to get up an hour early to be lectured by their boss was not the way any of the boys counselors intended to start their morning. Brad was the one to knock on cabin No.20's door.

"Get up Milton." he said. "You heard Ms. Cathy."

Milton walked over to the door in his boxers and a t shirt as he rubbed his eyes. "What's goin' on?" he said.

"A sister from St. Agatha's said she saw some boys leaving

her camp a few nights ago. We have to line you guys up to see if she can recognize anyone." Everyone in the cabin felt their hearts dropped into the pit of their stomachs. "So get dressed and head to the field." Brad said. Milton turned around and looked each of his cabin mates in the face.

"Aw man. What if she recognizes us?" Ralph groaned.

"How's she gonna know our faces?" Nicky said. "Our backs were to her the entire time."

"Me and Milton are two out of the only six black boys here." Ralph said.

Nicky jumped down from his bed. "If she saw one of you then she saw all of us. At least two."

"And besides, it was like two days ago." Johnny added. "Let's just get dressed and go."

When all of the boys from camp arrived at the field they were lined up. Everyone could see the anger in Ms. Cathy's face. Had she been able to clench her bullhorn any tighter she would have broken the handle. The sister from St. Agatha's was standing right beside her with a much older nun standing behind the both of them. Both sisters looked equally upset. Ms. Cathy leaned back as the younger nun whispered something into her ear.

Ms. Cathy put the bullhorn up to her mouth, "It has been brought to my attention that four of you were seen on St. Agatha's premises a few nights ago," she said. "That results in an immediate dismissal from Camp Hope N' Oak." Ms. Cathy paused as the sister whispered something else into her ear. "Luckily Sister Mary does not recognize the campers." The boys from cabin No.20 looked at each other as they all let out a collective sigh of relief.

"If any of you are spotted outside of the camp's premises you will be sent home immediately." Ms. Cathy said. "Your parents sent you all here to enjoy your summer in a fun and safe environment. I can not guarantee your safety if you are snooping around the woods after lights out."

When Ms. Cathy and the nuns left the field Brad took center stage. "As the assistant director and head of all counselors I will be administering the punishment. Who knows who snuck out the other night?"

All of the campers looked around at each other. "Since no one knows or is willing to confess who snuck out the other night, all of you are to stand here in silence until breakfast." Brad looked down at his watch, "That gives you guys a little under an hour." All of the boys groaned as Brad happily took a seat in a lawn chair.

Later that morning as the boys from cabin No.20 enjoyed their breakfast, Dylan Ricketts joined them at their table. "Hey can I sit here?" he said. He squeezed his way in-between Ralph and Johnny.

"What's goin' on?" Nicky said.

"You guys know Dennis Worthy?" Dylan asked. Everyone shook their heads yes. "Well he's been walking around all morning talking about how he and Milton got into this fight about a week ago."

"So what?" Nicky said.

"I'm getting to that." Dylan looked at Milton, "He's been saying he kicked your ass."

Milton stood up, "What?" he yelled.

"Hey sit down." Nicky said as he pulled Milton back into is seat.

"What he been sayin'?" Milton said with a concerned tone.

"He said you pushed him. Then he punched you knocking you down. Then he got on top of you and punched you until Brad broke it up."

"That's what I did to him." Milton pleaded.

"Not the way he's telling it." Dylan said. "I'd say you fight him again in front of witnesses."

"No," Ralph interjected, "if Milton gets in trouble again he's getting sent home."

"Too bad." Dylan said. "A lot of girls are talking about Milton getting beat up by Dennis. Especially the black ones." Milton stood up to see if Dennis was in the mess. When he realized Dennis wasn't there, Milton shoved his chair back and stormed out of the mess.

"See what you did?" Ralph said. "Now we have to find Dennis before Milton does." Ralph and Johnny left the mess in pursuit of

Milton. When Ralph and Johnny caught up to him they tried to dissuade him from looking for Dennis. Ralph tried to tell him that it wasn't worth it and that everyone who saw the fight knew what really happened although it was only several campers. None of what Ralph was saying was getting through to Milton. Johnny even tried stepping in front of him only to be pushed to the ground.

Ralph pleaded with Milton, "Why does it even matter?" he said. "You don't have to impress anybody." Milton stopped walking.

"It ain't about impressin' nobody. It's about my reputation." Everyone around camp knew Milton as one of the tough kids. He wasn't going to let some uppity punk undo all of that. " I'm whoopin' his ass and I don't give a damn if I get sent home." Milton Stormed off leaving Johnny and Ralph in the middle of the trail. About an hour before lunch Nicky went back to the cabin. When he got there Milton was sitting on his bunk donning an angry scowl.

"You still upset about that Dennis thing?" Nicky said.

Milton didn't say a word as he continued to stare at the cabin's window. "You still gonna fight him?" Nicky asked.

Milton hesitated before he gave an answer. "I don't know yet."

Nicky walked over to Milton, "I say you leave it alone. All of the guys know you beat him up and girls don't know anything." Milton hoped Nicky was right. He couldn't allow his reputation at camp to be ruined by a lie.

Across camp Johnny and Ralph were still looking for Dennis. Since trying to stop Milton failed they figured that if they could get to Dennis before Milton did that any further conflict could be avoided.

As they continued their search Johnny asked Ralph a question. "Hey Ralph. Do you think we'll ever find the counselor's hangout?" he said.

"I don't know and I really don't care. If that sister recognized us we would all be at home getting chewed out by our parents right now."

Johnny didn't agree with Ralph but he understood why Ralph felt that way. Ralph and Johnny stopped by the Leisure Hall to see if Dennis was in there. When they got inside Dennis was surrounded by several other campers. They were all circled around him as they listened to his fabricated story of his and Milton's fight. Ralph and Johnny saw why Dylan made the situation sound as bad as he did. Dennis' story had really begun to pick up steam. Ralph angrily marched over to Dennis.

"Hey Ralph," one of the campers said, "you hear about what Dennis did to Milton?"

Ralph grabbed Dennis and pulled him to the side. "Why are you telling everyone you beat up Milton?"

"Why not? I deserve to ruin his reputation after what he did to me."

"Don't you know that he knows you've been running around here lying?" Ralph's voice was full of concern.

"He can't touch me. If he does he'll get kicked out." Dennis said.

Johnny interjected, "This is Milton Williams we're talking about. You think he cares about getting kicked out?" Dennis thought about it for a second. Johnny had made a valid point. Milton had grown quite a reputation in the first few weeks of camp.

Dennis stood back and spoke loud enough for everyone in the room to hear. "I don't care. And go tell Milton he can have a rematch after lunch." Everyone in the room except for Johnny and Ralph erupted into cheers. Ralph tried to diffuse the situation but Dennis' own pride was blinding him. When word got back to Milton he couldn't wait until lunch. In his mind, Milton was going to go down in Camp Hope N' Oak infamy.

Everyone at camp was waiting to see if Dennis would show up to the mess for lunch. As the campers continued to flow in, the boys from cabin No.20 anxiously waited to see what their cabin mate Milton was going to do. When Dennis finally walked into the mess everyone went quiet. The counselors all looked around at each other in amazement. the mess was never this quiet at meal time. Milton stood up on top of his table. "Hey get down from there!" one of the counselors yelled out.

Milton didn't move. "I heard Dennis say he beat me up a couple of days ago. I want him to say it right here right now to my face." All attention shifted to Dennis as he remained silent. "Well nigga say it!" Milton said. Brad walked over to Milton and asked him to get down from on top of the table. Ms. Cathy ordered Brad to take Dennis and Milton to her office.

When Ms. Cathy got to her office she slammed the door shut. "What do you two have to say for yourselves?"

Dennis nervously blurted out the first answer he could think of. "Milton punched me in the face the other day. I wanted to tell you but Brad said everything was ok." Ms. Cathy looked over at her son who was in total disbelief.

"When were you going to tell me about my campers fighting?" she said.

"I didn't think it was necessary. I resolved the issue. Look mom, Dennis called Milton out of his name. Milton was just defending himself."

Ms. Cathy turned her attention back to Dennis and Milton. "Is this true?" Milton shook his head yes. "Here at Camp Hope N' Oak we don't condone violence nor do we condone name calling and disrespect. If either of you end up in my office again I will send you home. Do you understand me?" Both boys agreed. "Good. Now the two of you head back to the mess. Brad you stay here."

On the walk back to the mess neither of the boys said a word to each other. Before they got inside Milton blocked Dennis from opening the door. "Look man," he said, "I don't like you and my cabin mates don't like you. Ralph don't like you either my nigga. Don't talk to us, don't say hi to us, don't even mention any of our names or we will be gettin' sent home." Milton opened the door and went back inside to join his cabin mates leaving Dennis outside.

Valerie

By late July the dog days of summer were in full swing. The temperature reached well into the 90's on an almost daily basis. Every morning campers woke up drenched in sweat leaving their linens damp. On the hottest of days a trip from the cabins to the mess felt like a journey across the Sahara. The ceiling fans in the mess helped with the circulation of air but did little to keep the room cool. After breakfast a vast majority of the campers would spend their day at the lake trying to keep cool.

Ms. Cathy decided it was best to leave the mess open in between meal times so that the campers could have immediate access to water to prevent any of them from becoming dehydrated. The meals that were prepped became relatively light and required minimal to no cooking. Breakfast was reduced to only cold cereal and oatmeal while lunch and dinner consisted of mostly cold cut sandwiches.

After word got around that a group of boys snuck out of camp, some of the other campers took to the woods for shade. It didn't help that the counselors had become fairly lax with their enforcement of the "Don't leave the camp grounds" rule. The medium sized manmade lake could only fit but so many campers at once. Eventually Ms. Cathy caught wind forcing her to close the lake for two days.

When she reopened the lake everyone at camp rejoiced causing it to once again fill up to capacity. Even if a camper couldn't swim just being able to let your feet sway through the water was enough relief to make you believe that your body was submerged in the lake.

Ralph sat and watched as everyone else splashed around and played in the lake. He wasn't in the mood for swimming or playing around in the water. When Milton noticed Ralph sitting on the ground leaning back on his hands, he got out of the water and walked over to where Ralph was sitting.

"Why you ain't in the water?" Milton said.

"I don't really feel like it." Ralph replied.

"I guess so." Milton sat down beside Ralph as droplets of water fell from his wet afro that had grown longer since the beginning of camp. "You see Johnny around? He been disappearin' lately after we leave the mess."

"Yeah. I noticed that too." Ralph said. "Who knows where he is."

"You sure you don't wanna hop in?" Milton said in a last ditch effort to get Ralph to join him.

"Yeah I'm sure." Milton shrugged his shoulders before running back into the lake. Ralph leaned back and gazed up at the sun as he shielded his eyes. He stood up and walked back to the cabin.

Johnny was being led through the woods while blindfolded. He wanted to ask questions but decided it was best to allow her to keep the surprise a secret. Johnny and Valerie had been sneaking off together for the past couple of weeks. They met at the lake during their first week of camp and grew to become close friends. He liked her and she liked him. Valerie Hallstead was a twelve year old girl from cabin No.9. She had green eyes with long brunette hair that was almost as messy as Johnny's.

With the over crowding at the lake Johnny and Valerie figured it was easier to sneak off into the woods to keep cool. Valerie led Johnny through the woods to a cliff that overlooked a calm river bed surrounded by a rolling green valley. She let go of his hand and asked him to follow her. Johnny could hear birds chirping as bugs and insects buzzed all around them.

"I found this place a while back." she said. "The water gets a lot more intense after it rains." Johnny was in awe of the beautiful scenery. The sky was clear with not a cloud in sight.

"It's beautiful," he said. "I've never seen anything like this before." Johnny sat on the ground pulling Valerie down next to him. She rested her head on his shoulder as the two of them enjoyed their moment of peace together. Johnny looked down at Valerie and saw that her eyes were closed. "You going to sleep?"

he asked.

"No," she said, "I'm just listening."

Johnny could hear, touch, see, and smell everything around him. He was tranquil. No counselors, no other campers, no arguing or bickering cabin mates, just him, Valerie, and nature. After sitting there for a while Johnny was ready to get back to camp. "We should get out of here," he said. Johnny helped Valerie up as the two of them walked back to camp.

The next day after lunch Johnny and Valerie met up to go to their new secret spot. Unbeknownst to them, Nicky and Ralph had been following them since they left the mess. "Hold it," Nicky whispered. He crouched down as he made his way towards some brush to better conceal himself.

"Is it them?" Ralph asked.

"I can't tell," Nicky said. "I'm pretty sure it's him. He's the only boy here with hair as long as a girl's."

As Nicky crept closer to get a better view his knee snapped a branch causing it to make noise. He stopped in his tracks and waited to see if Johnny and Valerie heard the branch snap. Neither Johnny nor Valerie reacted. Nicky could breathe a sigh of relief.

He turned around and crawled back to Ralph's position. "It's definitely Johnny." Nicky said. "I just can't figure out who the girl is." The two of them sat and waited for Johnny and the mystery girl to leave so they could follow Johnny back to the cabin and surprise him. When Johnny stood up Nicky and Ralph finally caught a glance of the mystery girl.

"Hey Nicky," Ralph said, "isn't that Valerie from cabin No.9?"

Nicky squinted as he tried to get a better look. "That is her. C'mon, let's follow 'em to see where they're goin." As Ralph stood up he unknowingly stepped on a piece of forest debris. This time the snap was loud enough to alert Valerie. She turned around to see what caused the noise. Before she could fully turn her head around Nicky quickly snatched Ralph down to keep Valerie from spotting either of them.

"What's up?" Johnny said.

"I thought I heard something." Valerie continued to look around.

"It was probably just an animal."

Nicky and Ralph silently watched Johnny and Valerie walk back to camp. "That was close." Ralph said.

"Yeah it was." Nicky said. "Let's head back to camp before somebody notices we're gone."

Later that night before lights out the boys of cabin No.20 were up talking. Nicky and Ralph had already informed Milton about what they found earlier that afternoon. Milton took it upon himself to playfully interrogate Johnny about his most recent whereabouts. He jumped down from his bunk and approached Johnny. "Hey

Johnny," he said, "where you been at man?"

Johnny was still completely oblivious to the fact that the rest of his cabin mates had discovered where he had been going for the past few weeks. "What do you mean?"

"Don't play dumb." Nicky said. "Me and Dickerson saw you sneak off into the woods."

"And we know who you was with." Milton said as Johnny's face turned red from embarrassment. "It's all over yo face." Milton added.

"All we wanna know is if she's your girlfriend or not." Nicky said. Johnny felt attacked. He looked at all three of his cabin mates.

"Ok. Me and Valerie like each other a lot. I'd like her to be my girlfriend but the reality is that after camp we won't get to see each other again. Happy?" Johnny angrily rolled over in his bed so that none of his cabin mates could see his face. Everyone in the cabin grew quiet as the crickets continued to chirp in the moon's twilight.

The next morning Ralph and Johnny went to breakfast together. Ralph explained to Johnny that none of the cabin mates meant anything in their teasing. As Ralph and Johnny ate breakfast together Valerie walked in with a few of her friends. Johnny looked over at her and smiled prompting her to smile back. After they finished eating breakfast Johnny met up with Valerie.

"Hey Val," Johnny said, "you think you wanna skip our outing today?"

"Is everything ok?" she said.

"Yeah. I just want to hang out with the guys today. I'll see you later on today though."

"Ok," she said. She shot Johnny a quick smile before the two went their separate ways.

Later that afternoon Nicky and Milton were playing in the field with a few other campers. In the distance they could see a few of the counselors frantically running towards the lake. Moments later Ms. Cathy was seen racing down the foot path in her cart. Intrigued by the sight the small group of boys rushed over to the lake to see what all of the commotion was about.

As campers and counselors alike made their way to the lake a large crowd had already convened. The scene felt grim as a few murmurs spread throughout the crowd. Milton looked for a familiar face before he spotted his friend Lawrence.

"Why everybody huddled up around here?" Milton asked.

"I think somebody drowned in the lake," Lawrence said.

"A camper?"

"I think so."

Ralph and Johnny were on their way to the lake to meet up with Valerie for a mid-afternoon swim. By the time they got there a crowd had already formed around the lake. It didn't take long for word to spread through the crowd that Valerie Hallstead from cabin No.9 had to be pulled out of the lake.

As the crowd continued to talk amongst themselves the sound of a siren blared from the entrance of the camp. Since the ambulance was too big to fit through the camp's entrance one of the boys counselors hopped in Ms. Cathy's cart to rush the paramedics to the lake. Brad tried his best to keep Valerie alive with mouth to mouth resuscitation until the paramedics arrived.

Milton turned to Nicky, "You think she's dead?"

"I hope not," Nicky said.

When the counselor returned with the paramedics the other counselors told the crowd of frightened on-looking campers to make room for the stretcher. The parting of the crowd was the first opportunity many of the campers got to see Valerie. The chatter and murmurs came to a halt when everyone saw her pale and lifeless body laying in the grass. One of the paramedics kneeled down to check her pulse.

"Alright she still has a slight pulse," he said.

The paramedic leaned in to continue the mouth to mouth resuscitation.

"What's her name?" the paramedic asked.

"Valerie." one of the counselors yelled out.

"Alright Valerie. Come on." He pumped her chest several times hoping the water in her lungs would come shooting out like a geyser. Everyone watched in horror as their fellow camper lay there fighting for her life. A few of Valerie's friends and cabin mates were huddled together crying and consoling each other as the paramedics fought tirelessly to save the young girl's life. "Come on young lady. Don't do this to me."

The paramedic leaned in one more time to try and resuscitate her. Everyone feared the worst. As the paramedics tried one more time they saw that there was nothing more that they could do. The paramedics, accompanied by Ms. Cathy and the counselor who rescued Valerie from the lake, rushed Valerie to the nearest hospital. Ms. Cathy waited until after dinner to tell everyone the news that Valerie Hallstead had died on the way to the hospital.

That night after lights out Johnny couldn't go to sleep. He got out of bed, put on his shoes and slipped his t-shirt over his head. As he snuck out of the cabin the sound of the door closing woke Ralph up. When he saw that Johnny's bunk was empty Ralph put on his socks and shoes to go after him. When Ralph caught up to Johnny he was walking down the foot path towards the lake.

Johnny sat on the pier and kicked off his shoes as he ran his fingers through his long messy hair. He laid down on his back and gazed up at the stars. Ralph gave it some time before joining his friend on the pier.

"You alright?"

"Not really." Johnny said. A moment of silence fell between

the two friends. "Val lived in peace you know?"

Ralph looked over at Johnny who was still gazing up into the stars. He couldn't understand how Johnny could remain so calm. Johnny was just waiting on the right time to say goodbye to Valerie.

"You know the best part about death Ralph?" Johnny said. Ralph who couldn't think of any good that would come out of death kept quiet. "It makes us appreciate life a little more than we did before."

Ralph looked at Johnny who was still fixated on the starry night sky. "Do you want me to leave you be?" Ralph said.

Johnny just shook his head and replied, "No. I need my best friend here with me for this." As a tear began to roll down Johnny's face Ralph sat down beside him and comforted his friend in his time of need.

Missed Steps

The cold air and soggy ground was beginning to tire the boys from cabin No.20. Milton was successful in convincing his cabin mates to sneak out in the dead of night to continue their search for the Counselor's Hangout. As the boys continued to truck through the mud Ralph went into his backpack and pulled out a map Nicky and Milton had stolen from Ms. Cathy's office earlier in the week.

"Let me see." Milton said as he snatched the map from Ralph. Milton looked the map over. "We gotta go this way."

"You don't even know how to read a map." Nicky said.

"Shut up nigga! Yes I do!"

"That word doesn't work unless the other person is black!" Nicky said.

Johnny stepped in-between the two of them. "Guys. Calm down," he said.

Ralph walked over to a downed tree and sat on it. When his butt hit the tree the moisture from the wood made the back of his pants wet. Too tired and exhausted to care Ralph sat on the wet bark and watched as Johnny tried to play mediator to a bickering Nicky and Milton.

"All you gotta do is follow the leader," Milton said. "Is that too hard?"

"But you don't even know what direction we're headed in." Nicky said.

Ralph interjected. "So we actually have a map and nobody knows where we're going?" he said. The boys had been wandering through the woods for well over an hour. Even if they were headed in the right direction the counselors were definitely back at camp by now.

Milton assumed that if he got his hands on an actual map of the surrounding area that it would be easy for him and his cabin mates to find the hangout. The lack of navigation skills and knowledge of the direction in which the hangout was located had finally taken its toll on the cabin's morale. Not only were they lost but they didn't even know how to get back to camp.

"I can't believe I let you guys bring me all the way out here again for nothing." Ralph said.

"I know where I'm goin'." Milton said under his breath.

Ralph got up from his spot on the downed soggy tree trunk. "If you did we wouldn't be lost." Ralph said. "How do we even get back to camp?"

Milton sat in silence as Nicky and Johnny scanned over the map with a flashlight. They located Camp Hope N' Oak's position on the map but couldn't figure out what direction the camp was in from their location. Ralph walked over to take a look at the map.

Ralph began to walk around with the map in hand occasionally lifting his head as he tried to pinpoint the direction in which he and his cabin mates should go. He looked to his cabin mates. They all saw Ralph as the smartest kid in the cabin if not the entire camp. Surely he could make sense of things.

"Since Milton never marked any reference points I can't figure out where we are." he said.

Johnny turned to Milton. "Do you know what direction we went in," he asked, "because then we could kind of retrace our steps."

Ralph threw his hands up in frustration. "That won't work. What if we went off track and didn't know it? What if he doesn't even know what direction we went in?"

"The least we can do is try. Don't just wig out man." Johnny said.

"But we're lost in the woods Johnny, maybe even a mile deep!"

Everyone was shocked at how upset Ralph had become. Ralph Dickerson was thought to be the one of the most calm and collected campers at Hope N' Oak. No one would ever have thought he was the type to lose his temper let alone with his own cabin mates. He stormed off on his own to take time to recollect himself away from his cabin mates.

Johnny sat down with the map and continued to look it over.

Less than a quarter of an inch above the camp's position was a small blue blob marking the camp's lake. "Alright then," Johnny said, "this is the back of camp and we left from our side of the camp." Johnny said as he pointed to the left of the camp's marker. As Johnny traced his fingers along the map he figured that if they hadn't gotten turned around then they could just take the route Johnny was marking. If the boys did in fact go off course like Ralph suggested then getting back to camp was going to be more difficult than Johnny thought. When Ralph got back he was a bit calmer but he was still visibly upset.

"Well I got one route," Johnny said. "You can look at it and see if you can think of anything else." Ralph walked over to Johnny and looked at the map.

"Let's just take your route." Ralph said. "I just want to get back to camp and go to sleep."

"Then it's settled. We'll go that way," Johnny said as he pointed ahead.

Ralph agreed with a simple head nod prompting Johnny to lead everyone back to camp. Milton had lost all authority over the cabin's mission. Milton didn't say much after Ralph criticized him for his poor navigation and planning. He had become so upset with himself that it was hard for him to look any of his cabin mates in the face. His own curiosity and arrogance had pushed Ralph over the edge but most importantly Milton put everyone in serious danger. They could have ended up roaming around the woods until daylight.

As the boys continued on their way back to camp they couldn't help but to notice a foul stench. Everyone kept on walking without saying a word about the smell. The further they walked the stronger the odor became. Nicky took the flashlight from Johnny in hopes of finding the source of the horrendous odor.

"What are you looking for?" Johnny said.

"I gotta know what the hell that smell is," Nicky said.

Nicky covered his mouth and nose with his shirt as he moved closer to the source of what was causing the odor. The other three boys stood back and watched as Nicky continued his search. Suddenly he stopped in his tracks almost dropping the flashlight out of his hand. "Guys, come look at this." Nicky's shaky voice caused alarm amongst his cabin mates. Milton and Johnny moved in closer to see what Nicky had discovered.

"Is that a dead body?" Johnny said.

"Man, somebody messed that nigga up good." Milton said

The body, which appeared to be that of an adult male had already began to decompose. His shirt was covered in blood and his shoes were missing. His face was beyond recognition and judging by the various wounds on his body the man might have been tortured before he died.

"What do we do?" said Johnny.

"We got two options," Milton said. "We either tell somebody and get in trouble for sneakin' out or we keep this between the four of us."

Ralph who hadn't spoken a word since he yelled at Milton stepped up. "I say we keep our mouths shut. We've made it this far without getting caught." The boys all nodded in agreement as Nicky made the sign of the cross. Nicky handed the flashlight back to Johnny as cabin No.20 continued on their way back to camp.

The next morning when Johnny woke up he looked at the clock on the cabin's wall and saw that it was past 8:30. He rubbed his eyes and looked around the cabin to see if anyone else was still sleeping. He looked right across from his bunk and saw that Ralph was already gone for breakfast. He stuck his head out and saw Milton's arm draped over the edge of his bunk.

When Johnny got out of bed he saw that Nicky was also sound asleep. "Guys get up." he said. "It's like 8:30. I don't want to miss breakfast." Nicky got up and began to get dressed while Milton stayed in bed. "Milton, get up man. Ralph left us." Johnny said.

Milton had trouble falling asleep after the boys got back to the cabin following their failed mission. He had been up all night thinking about what he could have done better so that he and his cabin mates wouldn't have gotten lost. Milton felt that since it was his idea to go looking for the counselor hangout that he was responsible.

Nicky stepped up onto Ralph's bed to make himself eye level with Milton. "You comin' to breakfast?"

"Yeah man. Gimme a second." Milton said. After Johnny and Nicky left the cabin to go to breakfast, Milton continued to think about everything Ralph said to him the night before. This was their second failed attempt at trying to find the Counselor's Hangout. With August quickly approaching Milton knew that his time to find the counselor's hangout was slipping through his fingers.

An American Game

The game of choice for the majority of the boys at Camp Hope N' Oak was football. The amount of boys who frequently played baseball quickly declined after Ms. Cathy made it mandatory that girls were to be included in the games. After the first week of camp a group of girls who wanted to play softball felt that it was unfair that the boys got to control who played on the diamond when both sexes could utilize it equally. This upset quite a few of the boys prompting most of them to either play football or find other activities to occupy themselves.

Nicky played baseball but he loved football as did Milton. Other than when the two of them were in the cabin, the field was where Milton and Nicky spent most of their time together. One afternoon a bunch of the boys from various cabins including Nicky, met up to organize the camp's first game of 11 on 11 football. The organizer of the game was Greg Holland of cabin No.25. After the meeting concluded Nicky met up with Milton back at the cabin to tell him about the game.

"So who all playin'?" Milton said.

"David Rickets for sure," Nicky replied, "everybody from cabins no.22 and 27."

There were so many campers hoping to be picked that Nicky couldn't remember them all. There was Jeremy Thomas of cabin No.19 who was the tallest kid at camp. At only 13 years old Jeremy stood 6'1" tall with a full frame earning him the nickname Chub back home. Stevie Jackson of cabin No. 24 was one of the dozen or so black campers at Hope N' Oak. He was the only boy at camp shorter than Nicky but he was also one of the fastest. The camper everyone was excited to see play was Alvin "Hush" Bryant of cabin No. 30. He got the nickname Hush because he never said much around camp. In fact, hardly anyone at camp even knew what his normal speaking voice sounded like.

Hush was highly sought after by anyone who was picked a captain. The counselors started calling him little Joe Namath because of how well he played. Nicky knew Hush from junior high football. Although their teams never played each other Nicky saw firsthand what Hush was capable of before either of them even walked into camp.

"So when is the game?" Milton said.

"Tomorrow at 2."

"Can't wait," Milton said. "Who made captain?"

"Greg Holland and Richard Wallace." Greg was no Hush Bryant but he was pretty good compared to Richard Wallace who was clearly a popularity pick.

"Rich from 28 is a captain?" Milton was baffled. "I should've went and put my name in. I'm way better than that kid. When they pickin' teams?

"After breakfast," Nicky said.

Milton didn't care which team he was on. A full game of 11 on 11 was what he had been waiting for all summer. Back home it was easy to get a game together. Milton and his friends would get a bunch of kids from other streets in the neighborhood and run games all day until the street lights came on. He watched some baseball but was never really a fan. The only reason he played was because it was a sport he was pretty good at.

When it came time for teams to be picked the next morning 40 of the 58 boys at camp showed up to the field. When word spread that the boys were planning a big football game Ms. Cathy sent Brad and another counselor over to help the campers organize the game. After what happened at the lake she figured it would be a good idea to have all of the campers watch and cheer their friends on during a friendly game of football. Richard and Greg stood at the front of the crowd facing the pool of hopeful players. Brad pulled a quarter out of his pocket, "Call it in the air," he said.

As the coin flipped off of Brad's fingers Greg called it. "Heads" he said.

When the quarter landed on the ground George Washington was staring back at Richard and Greg. "You want first pick or ball first," Brad said.

Greg thought about it for a moment. "First pick." he said.

"Greg gets first pick and Richard gets ball first."

With his first pick to no surprise Greg took Hush. Richard chose one of his cabin mates first. For Greg's second pick he chose Jeremy Thomas. Richard chose one of his neighbors from cabin No. 29 for his second pick. It wasn't until the fifth pick that Nicky was chosen by Greg and the seventh pick until Milton was picked by Richard. David Rickets was picked up by Richard along with Stevie from cabin No. 24 and Milton's friend Lawrence. With both rosters set the captains took their teams to opposite sides of the field to run a few practice plays before lunch.

During lunch Milton and Nicky shared some friendly trash talk. "Too bad we didn't get picked for the same team," Nicky said.

"Oh well. Just watch out for me. I might lay the big hit on you." Milton said.

Ralph walked over and sat down at the table with his lunch. None of his cabin mates had seen him since breakfast. In fact he had hardly been around for the past few days. After lunch Ralph would seemingly disappear all day until it was time for dinner. It took Milton and Nicky a while to notice since Ralph rarely went to the field to begin with. He would usually be reading in the Leisure Hall or back in the cabin. Ralph and Milton hadn't spoken to each other since they had gotten lost for the second time looking for the

Counselors Hangout.

"Where you been?" Nicky asked.

"I've been around."

"We haven't seen you in a while." Nicky said.

Ralph quickly changed the subject. "I heard you guys are gonna play a big football game today."

"Yeah," Milton said, "you shoulda came to the draft. You probably woulda got picked."

"Nah. You know sports isn't my thing," Ralph said

Milton scarfed down what was left on his plate as he talked with a mouth full of food. "Come to the field after you done eatin'. You should come watch the game."

"I'll think about it." Ralph said.

"Alright. See you later." Nicky said as he and Milton got up to go put their dishes in the bin.

the mess was just about empty when Ralph finished his lunch. There had been a few rumbles of thunder in the area but no one thought much of it. Ralph walked over to a window and saw a group of rain clouds swiftly moving in over camp. Shortly after, one of the counselors made an announcement over the camp's PA system informing all campers to remain indoors. A storm had been reported in the area suspending all outdoor activities. Ralph sat back down at the table and waited for the storm to pass. Nicky and Milton were stuck with the Rickets twins in their cabin.

"What if it rains all day?" David said.

No one paid him any mind. Milton knew the game wouldn't be rained out. Besides, football was a game meant to be played in the elements. Milton began to wonder why the game had even been postponed in the first place. It wasn't like everyone playing didn't know the consequences of playing in the rain. That was part of the allure of football in his eyes.

Game time was quickly approaching. The rain continued to come down showing no intentions of stopping anytime soon. The anticipation continued to build throughout camp. A few of the counselors were even placing bets amongst themselves and the campers. Almost an hour after the scheduled game time an announcement was made that the storm would lift around 4 p.m. There was a collective cheer throughout the boys' cabins.

Milton looked over at David, "Guess we gon get to play today," as they gave each other a fist pound.

"You guys are gonna lose," Nicky said. "We have a way better team. Greg, Jeremy Thomas and Hush. You guys can't win."

"We got all of the black kids in camp who play football." Milton said. "Y'all can't win."

"We'll see at game time." Nicky said.

When the rain stopped for good everyone at camp made their way over to the field. It was still very dreary as the thick gray clouds remained over the area. All of the spectators lined up along both sides of the field. When Ralph arrived he saw Johnny and Dylan Rickets standing next to each other and decided to join them.

"What are the teams?" Ralph said.

"Well Greg's main players are Jeremy Thomas, Hush, and Nicky." Dylan said. "And Richard's are pretty much Milton, Stevie and my brother."

"Richard's got all of the black kids," Johnny said. "I'm cheering for them."

Ralph looked at both rosters and realized that Johnny was right. "I guess we're all cheering for Richard's team," Ralph said.

Just about everyone from camp was in attendance. Some of the girls led by a few of the counselors came up with cheers during the course of the game. The ground was muddy and the clouds continued to linger over camp. Richard's team was set to receive the ball first. The rules were simple. No first downs or punts and scoring a touchdown was the only way to score. First team to three touchdowns won. Instead of a kick off Brad threw the ball off to the receiving team.

Brad launched the ball down the field as Milton caught it and fielded it. Richard called the plays while David played quarterback. "Hand the ball off to Milton for the first play," Richard said. The huddle broke as everyone went to line up. "Go!" The center hiked the ball to David who handed it off to Milton. He ran for a big gain as the crowd erupted into cheers. When Milton stood up his entire front side was covered in mud.

Richard walked over to David to give him the next play. "I want Stevie to go deep," he said. On "Go" David dropped back and let the ball fly. Stevie tried to run under the ball but couldn't gain enough traction to catch up to the pass as it sailed over his head.

"Third down!" Brad yelled from the sideline. When everyone got back to the huddle Richard called another passing play. This time he was the primary target. As Richard went for the ball Greg jumped in front of him intercepting David's pass. On their first play from scrimmage Hush handed the ball off to Jeremy Thomas. Jeremy broke through a couple tackles before being wrestled to the ground by Milton and one of his teammates.

"C'mon y'all. Let's stop these dudes," he said in an attempt to rally his troops.

The next play Hush dropped back and saw Nicky running up the left sideline. He threw the ball to him completing the pass for a touchdown. The spectating campers continued to cheer while Greg's team celebrated in the end zone. Milton returned Brad's throw off for a long gain. After the play he walked to the huddle. "Rich, you gotta give me the ball."

"Alright" Richard said, "throw Milton the ball." Both teams lined up. David dropped back and waited for Milton to get open. When he let the ball go Jeremy Thomas tipped it.

Milton was irate on his walk back to the huddle. "David! What the hell man?"

"I'm sorry. I didn't see him."

"Just hand me the damn ball!" Milton yelled.

The teams lined up again. David handed the ball off to Milton who took off running. Jeremy Thomas squared his shoulders before laying a big hit on Milton causing the ball to pop out. When Milton stood up one of Greg's players had recovered the fumble. Greg ran into the huddle as he tapped his teammate on the butt. "Good job knocking the ball out of that nigger's hands Chub." Milton heard what Greg said while walking back to his team's huddle.

Milton looked around to see if anyone else had heard what Greg said. When he realized no one did, Milton's hunger to win grew. Everything was beginning to make sense to Milton. The picking of teams was no coincidence. Greg purposely picked an all white team. "Set! Hike!" Hush called out from behind center.

He handed the ball off to Jeremy who pulled five players on his back before he was brought down. Milton walked over to his friend and teammate Lawrence. "Get Greg," Milton said. Without hesitation Lawrence shook his head yes. Lawrence wasn't as big as Jeremy but he was a big boy in his own right.

Greg's team lined up as Milton walked over to Stevie's position. "Get Greg," he said.

"Why?" said Stevie.

"Cause he gettin' the ball."

"Set! Hike!" Greg took off into open space. Hush threw the ball to him as quickly as he could. After he caught it, Greg turned around and pitched the ball to Nicky. When Nicky caught the ball he followed all of his blockers into the end zone to extend his team's lead.

"Two to nothing, Greg's team," Brad announced.

Milton angrily marched over to Richard. "I'm returnin' it." he said.

Greg turned to the girls who were cheering for his team and winked. Everyone at the field had become emotionally invested in the game. Even Ms. Cathy and the counselors were applauding the boys Herculean efforts out on the soaked and muddy field. Ralph, Johnny and Dylan anxiously watched as everyone began to increasingly cheer more for Greg's team. "I hope they can do something." Dylan said.

Back on the field Brad threw the ball off. Milton caught it deep in the end zone. He got a good block from Lawrence before taking off up the sideline for a score as the crowd cheered him on. "We have a game" Brad said, "2 to 1."

Greg's team lined up for the throw off. Nicky caught the ball returning it to mid field. The offense huddled up. "Alright guys, this is for the game. Put it up top to me. I'll go get it," Greg said.

The teams lined up. At the snap Lawrence broke through the line forcing Hush to scramble. He avoided the sack before throwing the ball up field to Greg who couldn't get a hold of the wet and muddy ball. Greg dropped the pass as the crowd groaned. Greg slowly walked back to the huddle with his head down.

"Give it to Jeremy," he said. Hush handed the ball off to Jeremy. Lawrence broke through the line with a few of his teammates to successfully gang tackle Jeremy.

"Third down!" The momentum was now in Milton and Richard's team's favor. With only two more stops to go they would get the ball back with the opportunity to tie the game up at 2 - 2.

"Lock it up." Richard called out to his team.

Milton relayed the message, "Lock it up!" He hadn't forgotten what Greg said earlier. It was taking Milton everything he had not to lash out as the incident replayed over and over in his head. He wanted to lay a big hit on Greg before it was all said and done. Greg's team made their way up to the ball. "Let's go!" Milton said. The center snapped the ball to Hush who handed it off to Greg. Milton tried his best to avoid the blocks.

"Get him," someone yelled from the crowd.

Greg was finally brought down about ten feet from the goal line. His team huddled around him as he made the call. Milton, who had gained Richard's trust during the course of the game called out the assignments on defense.

"Lawrence, I want you on Jeremy. Stevie, you check Nicky. I got Greg." Both teams lined up. Hush dropped back before throwing a short pass to Greg as Milton hit a full sprint. Just as Greg caught the ball Milton lowered his shoulder and delivered a big hit on Greg. The crowd collectively groaned at the gruesome hit, "Ooohh…". Greg held on to the ball but was stopped just short of the goal line.

"Turnover. Richard's ball." Brad said.

Milton was elated. Laying that big of a hit on Greg gave him and the team a much needed morale boost. On the next play the center hiked the ball to Richard who gave it off to Milton who advanced the ball to mid field. When the team got back to the huddle Milton called the play. "Put it up top Rich. Me or Stevie gon' be there."

Richard nodded in agreement. "You heard him. I'm airing this one out." The huddle broke. Greg covered Stevie and Nicky took Milton.

"You crazy if you think we losin this one." Milton said

"No way man." said Nicky. "This is our game."

Stevie had been using his size to his advantage all day. He made a few good blocks by getting low and throwing opponents out of their lanes. On this play he chose to run in between all of the defenders and receivers to throw Greg off of his trail. When the ball was snapped Jeremy Thomas broke through the line, but not before Richard found Stevie wide open in the middle of the field. He threw the ball as best he could while absorbing the hit from Jeremy. Stevie caught the ball as he back peddled into the end zone.

"Touchdown Richard's team. We're knotted up at 2- 2. Next score wins." Brad said.

The crowd was stunned. Richard and Milton's team had captured all of the momentum after being down two touchdowns. All they had to do was stop Greg and his team of juggernauts. Both teams got ready for what could possibly be the last throw off of the game. Brad threw the ball downfield. Nicky dropped the ball before picking it up off of the ground and running for a few yards. The teams lined up before Jeremy Thomas took the handoff from Hush and rumbled for a big gain. The next play was a short pass to Greg who was stopped almost immediately by Milton and one of his teammates.

"Third down! Greg's team!"

Jeremy took the handoff from Hush and rumbled for another gain. Greg's team was within striking distance. Every player on the field was exhausted and covered in mud. Dozens of other campers in the crowd had been splashed with mud over the course of the game. The clouds continued to linger as both teams lined up for what could possibly be the end of the game. Hush dropped back looking to pass the ball. His first option was Nicky but Stevie had him completely covered.

As Milton scanned the field he saw Jeremy trying to get past David Rickets well short of the end zone. When Milton looked around to find Greg he saw him running towards the end zone uncovered. Milton turned and ran in Greg's direction. At the last moment Hush threw the ball up hoping Greg would make the catch. Milton jumped into the air reaching out for the ball hoping to break up the pass. As the ball began to fall Greg reached his hands out over Milton's and caught it. As Greg fell to the ground with possession of the ball the crowd's cheers were deafening.

"3 - 2. Final, Greg's team." Greg got up and ran over to his teammates as they celebrated with a crowd of excited campers. Milton who was still sitting on the ground looked at the opposing team and dropped his head in disappointment. Brad made his way over and kneeled down beside Milton. "You played a hell of a game out there. Don't be so down."

After everyone had already left the field Milton was still sitting in the same spot where he failed at trying to stop Greg from catching the game winning pass. Realizing their cabin mate was collecting himself, Ralph, Johnny and even Nicky stood on the sideline until Milton was ready to go. Milton had suffered a much greater loss than the one out on the field.

Before We Go Home...

When Nicky heard the cabin door close it woke him up. Nicky groggily looked around the dark room to make sense of what was going on. Nicky looked down and saw Ralph climbing into his bed. Seeing no cause for alarm Nicky closed his eyes and went back to bed.

The next morning when Nicky woke up to get dressed for breakfast he saw Ralph had already left for the mess. Nicky wanted to ask Ralph what he was doing out so late the night before. Instead of spending his day tracking Ralph down, Nicky went on with his day as usual. He ate breakfast with the Rickets twins before meeting with Milton over at the field. After lunch Milton asked Nicky if he wanted to be his partner in the foosball tournament taking place in the Leisure Hall later that evening. To keep Milton from getting involved with his interrogation of Ralph, Nicky had to think of an excuse to get rid of Milton.

"Sure," Nicky said. "I'll be over after I finish somethin'."

"What you gotta do?"

"Don't worry about it." Nicky said. "I'll see you in a little bit."

Once he got back to the cabin Nicky found Ralph sitting on his bed reading a copy of *Catcher in the Rye*. "What's goin' on?" Nicky said.

"Nothing much." Ralph replied.

Nicky didn't want to give himself away too early. He had to figure out a way to ease last night into the conversation. He started with the most obvious clue.

"Where'd you get that book from?" Nicky said.

"Out of the library."

Nicky knew Ms. Cathy wouldn't put that book in the camp's library. He was already beginning to trap Ralph in his own lie. "You don't say. I'd find it hard to imagine Ms. Cathy puttin' a book like that into the library."

Nicky's observation caught Ralph by surprise. He tried to throw Nicky off of his trail. "It was in there. You just had to look for it." he said.

"I read more than just comics Ralph. I spend a lot of time in the library. I can tell you for a fact that *Catcher in Rye* was never in there."

Ralph was becoming annoyed with Nicky's interrogation. "What's your point?" Ralph said.

"I saw you last night and I wanna know where you went."

Ralph had been found out. He closed the book and sat upright.

"Alright." he said. Nicky sat down across from Ralph on Johnny's bed. "Remember that girl we met the first night we went looking for that hangout you and Milton were talking about?" Nicky nodded his head yes. "Well…" Ralph paused for a moment. "That's where I was coming from last night."

Ralph's reveal took Nicky by surprise. He couldn't believe Ralph snuck out of the cabin at night alone to go see the girl from St. Agatha's. Especially when Ralph had been the most adamant about the possibility of getting caught sneaking around camp after lights out.

"I didn't think you were the adventure type." Nicky said. "Why'd you go back to see her anyway?" Ralph began his story from the beginning.

After the night cabin No.20 stumbled upon St. Agatha's, Ralph couldn't stop thinking about Jess. He wanted to see her again but didn't know exactly how he would go about doing so. A few weeks after the sisters form St. Agatha's came to notify Ms. Cathy of their camp's intruders, Ralph began to hatch a plan to get back to St. Agatha's. Since Ralph spent a great deal of his day alone he figured no one would even notice that he was gone.

He kept a low profile and had alternate routes leading into the woods in the case that his preferred route, past the field and diamond, was too busy. One day after lunch Ralph waited until he was all alone. Since the lake was closed Ralph's preferred route would be too congested for him to make his exit.

He went to the Leisure Hall and waited for his opportunity to sneak off into the woods from there. Thanks to the daylight Ralph easily found his way through the woods to St. Agatha's. Taking cover behind a tree Ralph patiently hoping that he would spot Jess walking to her dorm. After waiting for nearly an hour Ralph was ready to head back to camp. Just before he got up to leave Ralph saw Jess walking with two other girls.

Ralph's heart began to race as his palms grew clammy. He waited for his chance to emerge from the cover of the trees. When the coast was clear Ralph rushed over to Jess' dorm. He peeked through one of the back windows to see if anyone was downstairs. When he saw that the downstairs was clear Ralph opened the back door and made his way into the dining room and past the long mahogany table to the stairs.

Suddenly he heard a group of girls coming down the stairs Ralph ran back as quickly and quietly as he could into the other room. After he heard the front door close he proceeded to go upstairs. As he tiptoed through the hallway Ralph poked his head into every open door he could in hopes of finding Jess. Before he took a peek into the final room at the end of the hall Ralph felt a tap on his shoulder. When he turned around it was Jess.

Nicky couldn't believe what he was hearing. All of this time he thought of Ralph only as a nerdy bookworm. In reality he was a normal kid just like everyone else at camp. "Never thought you had it in you Dickerson." Nicky said.

By lights out, Ralph and his cabin mates were all in bed. Ralph waited patiently until everyone was asleep. After about an hour of silently laying in bed and pretending to be asleep Ralph sat up. First he checked to make sure that all of his cabin mates were asleep starting of with Johnny. When Ralph could see that Johnny was fast asleep he slowly got out of bed. Ralph stood up and looked at both Nicky and Milton. He was relieved to see both of the night owls were also sleeping. Ralph quickly got dressed and grabbed his backpack which he had filled with snacks before quietly sneaking out of the cabin.

With map and flashlight in hand Ralph began his trek through the dark and dense woods en route to St. Agatha's. Two months prior you couldn't pay Ralph Dickerson to sneak out in the middle of the night. But here he was in the dead of night, solely off of faith, to go meet with Jess. When Ralph made it to the tree line bordering St. Agatha's he checked his watch and waited for Jess to come out. As he anxiously waited Ralph's mind began to wander. "What am I doing here," he thought to himself. "What if she's asleep? Then I snuck out and risked all of this for nothing."

Finally he heard the back door open up as Jess poked her head out to make sure that the coast was clear. She was wearing light makeup and had a saddle bag draped over her shoulder. Ralph's face lit up as he raised his flashlight and flickered it twice to get Jess' attention. Jess was just as happy to see Ralph as he was to see her. She jogged over to him to keep from being seen. "Should we get going?" Jess said.

"Uh… yeah," Ralph said nervously. "I brought sodas and snacks too if we get hungry or thirsty."

"Cool." Jess said. "So where we headed?"

"A secret place that only a few people know about."

"Where is it?" Jess said. She was giddy and full of excitement.

"Not too far from here."

This was the happiest Ralph had been all summer, although he was kicking himself for waiting until the end of camp to see Jess again. He led Jess to a patch of grass where a beam of moon light shined through the canopy illuminating the area where the two of them were sitting.

"Potato chips or a cup cake?" Ralph said as he rummaged through his backpack.

"No thank you. I'll take a soda if you have one though."

Ralph reached into his backpack to show Jess her options. "Sure. I have cola and orange."

"Cola is fine." she said.

Ralph opened the can of cola and handed it to her. There was a brief moment of awkward silence between the two of them as they both tried to figure out something to say.

"So what do you have planned when you get back home?" Jess said.

"I'll probably just lay around until it's time to go back to school. What about you?"

Jess had been twiddling with a blade of grass between her fingers. "Probably the same thing." she said.

"I'm glad camp is almost over. I'm beyond sick of this place." Ralph said.

"I've been sick of being here. At least you don't have to pray six times a day."

"That's true." Ralph said. "So is this a Catholic School or something?"

"Yeah. We're all going to high school this year. This is supposed to be our summer bonding experience before we start school."

St. Agatha's summer camp prepared the girls for the curriculum of the school. The girls got up every morning at 6 a.m. except for on Saturdays when they didn't have to be up until 7 a.m. The girls had to be dressed and at the dinner table of their respective dorms by 6:15. After breakfast which ended promptly at 7 a.m. the girls went to class like a regular school day where they studied Bible scriptures, English, and math. After school some of the girls had to go to the chapel where they practiced singing for the school's chorus. There was also a small music conservatory where other girls would learn to read, write, and perform classical secular music.

Before they ate dinner the girls' dorms had to be swept, mopped, and dusted. The chapel and conservatory were also to be cleaned daily. If your dorm was chosen to prepare dinner then that meant that you and your dorm mates also had to help the sisters clean the kitchen that night. After dinner the girls attended a night prayer in the chapel before going to bed by 8. Their weekends were spent praying and cleaning and doing light landscaping around the campus including mowing the lawn, cleaning leaves, and garden work.

"This place is like a death camp compared to where you guys are." Jess said. "Plus it's all girls so that sucks even more."

"When do you get to go home?" Ralph said.

"Only two more days, thank God. I can't believe I've been here for the entire summer."

"Yeah. Me either." Ralph said. He was masking his disparity behind the tone of his voice. He began questioning why he never had the courage to come see Jess earlier.

"You still got some snacks in that bag? I haven't had junk food in months." said Jess.

Ralph couldn't continue kicking himself over the past. All he do was appreciate the time he had now. After a while Ralph wasn't even listening to Jess. He was too busy reveling in her beauty. He adored her smile and he loved it whenever she used her hand to brush her long red hair out of her face and behind her shoulder.

Besides his cabin mates, Jess was the only person Ralph had connected with over the course of the summer. He was becoming increasingly upset about Jess leaving in a few days, but Ralph knew there was nothing he could do about it.

"Why'd your parents even send you here?" Ralph said.

"So I don't end up like my older sister."

"What happened to her?" Ralph was trying to get to know Jess as much as possible before it was time to leave.

"She left home with her boyfriend for San Francisco a few years back when she was 16. She doesn't talk to them much and I have to sneak and call her."

"Milton's brother is fighting over in Vietnam so I can understand you missing your sister."

"Yeah." Jess said as she let out a sigh.

After more conversation Ralph and Jess had eaten all of the snacks Ralph brought with him. He checked his watch. "We should get going." he said in a melancholy tone.

"Yeah we should." Jess didn't sound too enthused about leaving either.

When the two made it back to St. Agatha's Jess stopped and turned to Ralph. "Well this is me," she said followed by another awkward silence. "I really had fun."

Ralph looked at her smiling form ear to ear. "I did too." he said.

"Oh yeah I almost forgot." Jess pulled a book out of her saddle bag. "Here you go. I think you'll like it." It was a copy of J.D. Salinger's *The Cather In the Rye.*

"Thanks." Ralph said. "I always wanted to read this book but I-."

Jess gave Ralph a peck on the cheek leaving him speechless. She waved goodbye before heading back in her dorm. Ralph watched Jess walk all the way to her dorm until she got inside.

As Ralph made his way past the Leisure Hall he thought he could hear indistinct chatter accompanied by a few giggles. In the distance he could see several dark figures walking past the camper's cabins. Realizing that the figures were the counselors returning from their secret hangout, Ralph waited until the coast was clear before hurrying back to his cabin.

After he got inside Ralph hopped into his bed. He was having trouble falling asleep and already missed Jess. There was nothing more he could do. Ralph pulled out *The Catcher in the Rye* and began to read it. As Ralph finished telling his story, Nicky began connecting the dots.

"You figured out where the hangout is." Nicky said.

"I did?" Ralph said confused.

Nicky stood up and went under his pillow. He pulled out the map he and Milton had stolen out of Ms. Cathy's office. "We're gonna find that hangout before we go home," Nicky said, "and it's all because of you." Ralph was still lost. He walked over to the map and looked it over as everything started to make since. When Ralph told Nicky that he saw the counselors sneaking back into camp Nicky finally figured out which direction the hangout was in. Nicky gave Ralph a stern pat on the back as he congratulated him. "Good job Dickerson." Nicky said.

The Things They Learned

One morning after Milton woke up he saw that he was the person to get up for breakfast. He got out of bed, got dressed, and walked over to the mess for breakfast. By the time he got there most of the other campers were already finished eating. The best a camper could do when he or she was late to breakfast was a glass of orange juice and a few slices of toast or a bagel. Milton had a much different experience during his summer at Camp Hope N' Oak.

He was lucky that both Mr. Tommy and his assistant Carl were black. Whenever Milton was late to breakfast Mr. Tommy would put a plate to the side for him. Breaking the rules for one of his own outweighed the risk of his boss finding out. In Mr. Tommy's mind if he didn't look out for the dozen or so black campers at Hope N' Oak, then who would? Mr. Tommy especially liked Milton. The two had forged a pretty close bond throughout the course of the summer. Milton was plenty tough with a slick mouth to boot. Milton reminded Mr. Tommy of himself when he was that age.

Milton casually strolled into the kitchen as if he owned the place. He sat down on a stool as Mr. Tommy and Carl cleaned the Kitchen. Mr. Tommy took a break from cleaning the stove to hand Milton a covered plate. "Got you some bacon, a bagel and some oatmeal," he said. "We ran out of eggs pretty fast."

"Thanks Mr. Tommy," Milton said. Milton uncovered the plate and began devouring everything on it.

"You a lil' later than usual today."

Milton ate a few more spoonfuls of his oatmeal. "Been havin' trouble sleepin'."

"You just ready to go home is all. I remember when the Japs surrendered." Mr. Tommy said. "I couldn't sleep 'til we got back to the Sates."

"Did you miss all your friends when you got back from the war?" Milton said.

Mr. Tommy, who was hunched over the stove cleaning it stood straight up. "I keep in touch with two of 'em," he said. "Some died in Korea and the others I have no clue where they at." Mr. Tommy paused for a moment. "But if you care about a friend you should tell them. You never know when you'll get that chance again."

Milton finished his plate and thanked Mr. Tommy for the food and the advice. Milton's concern was less about leaving Camp and more about whether or not he was returning home with a successful mission. Sure he was going to miss Johnny, Nicky, and Ralph, but discovering the Counselors Hangout with the three of them would be a memory he could cherish forever.

Meanwhile Nicky had spent the entire morning following a few of the counselors around. He was hoping to find out when was the next time they would be going to their hangout. Like Milton, the success of Nicky's summer rode on him and his cabin mates finding the Counselor's Hangout. He also knew in order to find the hangout, it would take all four of his cabin mates working together.

First, there had to be a lookout. The counselors usually left an hour or so after lights out because they knew that most of the campers were asleep by then. Since Ms. Cathy drove home every night after dinner it was relatively easy for the counselors to sneak out in the dead of night for a few hours of smoking and drinking. If one of the boys could keep watch until the counselors left without being caught, then they could tell the others which direction the counselors went in when the coast was all clear.

When Nicky got back to the cabin Ralph was laying on his bed reading J.D. Salinger's *Catcher in the Rye*. "Have you seen Milton today?" Nicky said.

"Not since I left this morning and he was still sleeping. You check the field or Leisure Hall?"

"I checked everywhere. I can't find him." Nicky said. His

voice was full of frustration.

"I can tell him you're looking for him. Anything specific you want me to tell him?"

"Nah. I'll catch him eventually." Nicky got up and left the cabinet.

Later that night after dinner everyone headed back to their cabins to get ready for bed. Right before lights out Nicky took the floor. "Alright guys, I know we tried this a few weeks back and got lost, but this plan is full proof." Nicky pulled out the stolen map that now had several notes scribbled on it. As he unfolded the map everyone gathered around. "I found out that the counselor's hangout is past the lake."

"How'd you find that out?" Milton said.

"Dickerson saw them sneaking back into camp a few nights ago." Nicky said.

"Yeah but we don't know when or if they're going back to the hangout." said Ralph.

Milton interjected "I do." he said. "Next Thursday."

"How'd you find that out?" Ralph said.

"When I was late goin to the mess this mornin' I heard some of the counselors talkin' about they last hangout of the summer."

"Why next Thursday?" Nicky asked.

"Because the last day of camp is Friday." Johnny said.

The boys all looked around at each other. After being together for the past five weeks it finally dawned on the boys that their summer together at Camp Hope N' Oak was just about up. The realization of them leaving was sobering. No one said a word for a brief moment. "So we doin' this?" Milton said. Nicky looked Milton directly into his eyes and nodded yes.

"Sure, why not?" Johnny said as he shrugged his shoulders.

Ralph looked at each of his cabin mates as they anxiously waited for his answer. He finally understood what this mission meant to not only Nicky and Milton, but to Johnny and even himself. It wasn't about being deviant out of boredom. It had become about much more than that.

"I'm in," Ralph said. "Can't get in trouble on the last night anyway." They all rejoiced as planning for their final mission got underway.

Each ensuing day seemed to drag on for the boys of cabin No.20. There was a mixture of emotions as the boys dealt with their excitement of their last adventure paired with the overarching sadness of having to leave their friends the next day. cabin No.20 spent just about every waking moment of the final week together. Nicky and Milton even got Johnny and Ralph to play in a game of football. As the end of camp drew near the boys prepared to put their plan into motion.

As the crickets chirped in the dead of night Milton anxiously waited for the counselors to come out of their dorms. He sat quietly in the shadow of Ms. Cathy's office. After a while Milton finally saw the girls' counselors come out of their dorms.

Back at the cabin Johnny, Nicky, and Ralph waited for the boys' counselors to leave their dorm. Everyone could feel their stomachs begin to turn as tiny beads of sweat ran down each of their faces. Suddenly they heard some chatter coming from behind their cabin. The voices accompanied by footsteps caused everyone in the cabin to stop what they were doing.

"You think you can get her to go all the way tonight?" one of the voices said.

"I know I can." another voice replied.

Once the voices faded everyone finished getting ready. Two months prior, finding the Counselors Hangout was only a priority to Milton and Nicky. Tonight it was on everyone's agenda. Once the boys knew the counselors were gone they made their move. Like before Johnny and Milton snuck out first as Nicky locked the door behind them. Then he slipped through the cabin's back window before joining the others out front. The three of them tip toed across the trail to join Milton who was still hiding behind Ms Cathy's Office.

"Which way did they go?" Nicky said.

Milton pointed in the direction of the lake. "That way. Just like Ralph said."

"It's do or die time fellas," Nicky said. "Let's rock and roll."

With no one around to se them cabin No.20 casually walked through camp and into the woods. The further the boys made it into the woods the more their anxiousness subsided. During the course of their summer each of the boys in one way or another had become battle hardened. They knew where to go, what to do in the event that they got lost, and most importantly how to depend on each other. "Where's the flashlight?" Milton said. Ralph reached into his backpack and handed the flashlight to Milton.

"Don't keep it on too long." Ralph said. "We don't know how close we are to the counselors."

Suddenly the boys heard a couple of voices coming from up ahead. "Turn that off," Nicky said in a whisper. Milton quickly turned the flashlight off.

Completely open without cover the boys had to think of something quick. Johnny spotted a downed tree several feet away. "Over there." he said. Everyone scurried over to the large trunk and took cover. The voices continued to grow louder as everyone sat nervously waiting.

"They're coming this way." Ralph said in a whisper. He was full of panic. Johnny put his finger up to his mouth signaling Ralph to keep quiet. Johnny peeked from behind the rotted tree trunk to try and make sense of what was going on but it was too dark for him to see.

"You sure you want to do it here?" the female counselor said.

"Why not?" the male counselor replied. "No one is here and if you keep quiet no one will know." Milton and Nicky looked at each other. They both grew up with older brothers. Nicky wanted to laugh but he kept his composure. As the counselors began to kiss and get more intimate it became harder for Nicky to keep quiet. Milton put his hand over Nicky's mouth. As the female counselor began to moan Nicky let a small giggle.

"What was that?" the female counselor said.

The other counselor stopped what he was doing. "I didn't hear anything." he said.

"I swear I heard a giggle." she said.

"Maybe it was an owl."

"Tommy I know what I heard and it wasn't an owl. You better not have anyone watching us." she said.

"Shh," Tommy said. "Just listen."

Everything was quiet except for the sounds of the night. As the counselors began to go back at it Nicky looked at Milton with a slight grin. "That was close," Nicky whispered. Ralph was too nervous to be amused by sex as Johnny smirked and patiently waited for the counselors to finish.

"Oh Tommy," she moaned. " that feels so good." Nicky let out another giggle prompting him to cover his own mouth. This time no one laughed, not even Milton.

"That sounded like a kid." Tommy said. cabin No. 20's

116

position had been compromised. "Come out now and I won't tell Ms. Cathy when she gets back in the morning." Tommy looked around hoping that the campers would give themselves up. None of the boys moved a muscle. They knew the counselors would get in just as much trouble as they would for sneaking out at night. "Alright, new deal," he said. "We're leaving and you better leave too." Tommy and the female counselor got up and fixed their clothes.

"Let's get back to the bonfire." Tommy said.

"We can't leave campers out here." the other counselor said.

"The hell we can't. These little bastards snuck out here on their own. No one brought them out here." The counselors continued to bicker at each other as they marched back to where the rest of the counselors were.

The boys remained behind the tree for several minutes until they were sure the counselors were gone. "Hand me the flashlight." Johnny said while still keeping his voice to a whisper. He peeked around the tree and flickered the light twice before turning to his cabin mates.

"Coast is clear." he said.

"That was a little too close." Ralph said.

"That just mean we gettin close" said Milton.

Johnny took the lead as the boys proceeded deeper into the woods. The counselors didn't know it but they were leading the boys right to their hangout. The close call wasn't going to deter cabin No.20 from their main objective. The further they trekked the more their anticipation grew. The boys knew that they were getting closer to the hangout.

"Hold it," Johnny said. He could hear indistinct chatter that sounded as if it was coming from up ahead. Everyone frantically looked around for cover as the voices grew louder. Each of the boys found a tree to hide behind as the counselors got closer. Since he was so small, Nicky laid down well out of the way of the counselors' path. Johnny signaled everyone to stay low until the counselors passed by.

As cabin No.20 waited for the counselors to go by, Ralph saw a glimmer of light in the distance. He wanted to alert the others but first they had to deal with their current situation. Two counselors were headed in their direction. As the two counselors made their way towards cabin No.20's position one of them stopped to urinate.

"Hold in a sec. I gotta take a piss." one of the counselor's said. He stopped in front of the tree that Milton was using for cover. While the counselor relieved himself on Milton's tree the other counselor struck up a conversation.

"Guess what Tommy just told me." he said.

"What?" asked the other counselor.

"So him and Sammy are screwin' right? He said she starts to

hear some giggles so he stops."

"Giggles?" the other counselor said.

"Giggles. So he stops and gets her back into it. Next thing he knows he hears the giggles."

"So he got caught fucking by some kids? That's hilarious." As the counselor finished his bathroom stop he zipped up. The strong smell of counselor's beer laced urine made Milton want to gag.

"Let's hurry up and get back to check on the campers." one of the counselor's said.

The counselors continued talking until they were out of the area. When everything was clear they all stood up and dusted themselves off. Ralph who was still fixated on the glowing light up ahead alerted everyone else to his discovery. "Hey guys look up there." he said. Everyone turned their heads in the direction Ralph was pointing to. As the boys cautiously walked forward they began to hear someone playing a guitar up ahead.

Everyone was in disbelief. Their holy grail, the thesis of their summer was right in front of them. When they got as close as they could without being seen each of them took a seat on the ground. The counselors were all drinking and laughing as a few of them danced around the bonfire together.

As the boys watched the fire flicker in the distance Ralph took off his backpack and pulled out a soda. He passed the bag around as each of his cabin mates did the same. As the counselors celebrated the conclusion of their summer so did cabin No.20. They each cracked open their sodas as they shared a silent toast to a mission accomplished.

ABOUT THE AUTHOR

Brendan Whitt is an author, journalist, and screenwriter from Cleveland, Ohio. He first discovered his love of writing at the age of 13 when he took home first prize at the 2005 "Power of the Pen" competition for his district. Before graduating with a B.A. in Liberal Arts from Cleveland State University, Brendan published his debut novella *A Summer In Harlem*.

A Summer In Harlem tells the story of Thad, a teenager from Beloit Alabama, as he visits his aunt and three cousins in a decaying Harlem neighborhood during the summer of 1948.Brendan's writing has been described as an "unapologetic realism with an insightful perspective" of America seen through a "grit covered lens".

Brendan has also published two collections of poetry as well as several features for the Call & Post Cleveland. In his spare time Brendan likes to work on his screenwriting and plans to have a film produced in the near future. You can follow Brendan on Instagram, @sneakersmcgee, and follow or friend him on Facebook.

"Keep chippin away at that marble block until it becomes a statue"
- Young Langston